IRREGULARS

by
Marilyn Jacovsky

THE PERMANENT PRESS
Sag Harbor, New York 11963

Library of Congress Cataloging-in-Publication Data

Jacovsky, Marilyn.
    Irregulars / by Marilyn Jacovsky
       p. cm.
    ISBN 1-57962-018-3
    I. Title.
    PS3560.A2848I77 1999
    813'.54--dc21   98-34207
                                                    CIP

Dislclaimer: This is a work of fiction. Any resemblance to any persons living or dead is purely coincedental.

THE PERMANENT PRESS
4170 Noyac Road
Sag Harbor, NY 11963

Fourth printing, March 1999

*"Don't fold the pages," my mother would say.
"Books have feelings." I always remember this delicate
point. Especially when I lose my place because of it. I
still think of a corner as a significant part of a book's
anatomy, however small, however chaste. If not for this
excess, which on our own bodies we call fat, how else
could we turn the pages. In fact, there have been times
when I have bent a corner back, subjecting the little
white point to my overbearing will the way one twists a
skinny arm. In these moments, to my surprise, I have
heard a moan. It is a flat, almost inaudible sound that
could easily be mistaken for complete and utter resigna-
tion . . . The sound however, is my own. It is the sound
of guilt without logic.*

Note to reader: Please do not fold the pages.

IRREGULARS

MANY YEARS ago my father took me to the warehouse I now live in where he destroyed my taste for chicken. It was still dark when he woke me up to go to the "zoo." That was where the animals hung frozen inside out. I would play in the freezer with the hanging carcasses until he finished filling his orders for the week. This morning he had a special surprise for me though and I couldn't wait.

Wood flakes softened a hard floor, moistening it with the scent of the forest after the rain. "It is a special carpet for the chickens," said a big man who wore a bloody apron that tied from behind. "Well, are you ready for the surprise?" my father asked. "Now put your hands over your eyes till we say ready," they sang. "One, two, three," they shouted, "hands down!" The curtains unfolded as a chicken ran frantically across the room. "It's missing its head, it's missing its head," I cried, "and it has no eyes to look for it!" My father and the man with the bloody apron laughed all the way down a long dark hallway until they disappeared. The echo of their laughter bounced off the sanguine tiled walls while I was left behind with the chicken to look for its head. I was six years old then.

I had forgotten about the chicken until one day quite recently. I was walking down a cobblestone street in the Meat Market when I noticed how the entrails of so many chickens stuck in between the cracks. Unfortunately, I had already signed the lease to my loft. Since the epiphany, the chicken has not stopped running past my thoughts. Albeit, the head I now look for is my own . . . sometimes my clients.

Smelling a neighborhood before seeing it instills a

primitive loathing in most people, especially when it smells of dead meat. Malodorous scent is a regional handicap few residents ever triumph over. Yet, the investment of *trying* to transforms the smell, however rank, into a visceral encoding for "home, sweet home."

At night the Meat Market is spectacular. Peacocks with basketball players' feet vogue to the sound of honking horns. Iridescent clowns sell sad faces to strangers in old cars. Their flamboyant colors bounce off gray warehouses worn out by time. Below my window wigs go flying over bloody fights with Johns who bargained for one sex and got the other. Through flashing lights and police sirens that always come too late I sleep . . . No one cares who wins.

Across the street leather sadists search underground clubs for their other side. Whipped and chained, a union of untold hurts is made . . . young men with pierced nipples and swollen gonads are penetrated by the devil. Few words are said. Genetic males parade as women above ground while "real men" parody themselves with a vengeance below. Human plasticity is nowhere more extreme.

Elevated, rows of artists' lofts are boxed and visible through my window. From a darkened corner I study them. Silently, imperceptibly, I zoom in. I watch them work from behind. I know their process. The painter strokes his guitar in between stroking his canvas. There is an onanistic quality to the quick jerky movements of his fingers over the strings. He builds himself up this way until he cums in color over an oversized canvas. Then, with barely a twist in motion, I move on to the next loft in the row. A young woman with pencil erasers for nipples stares into an unframed mirror on her easel.

It's the last frontier. It's the Wild West. It's the place I call home. It is also my office. In a remote corner on the sixth floor I sit one to one, unraveling a puzzle that is driving a stranger mad. I don't know what I will find but there are no interruptions. Insulated from world I chance the need for rescue.

An empty chair sits in the center of my loft with arms extended like a skeleton left wanting. The canvases lean against the walls like men out of work. The art market has fallen to its knees and so has my art career. I paint in between clients. It's no secret. Fumes permeate the office. A touch of titanium white on my sleeve gives it away.

"To get blocked is a human condition," I tell a client, "it doesn't matter what the art. It happens in painting, in therapy, in life. The struggle is generic. Give me twenty associations to the word house . . . You see the first ten are like everyone else's. It's only when you start to grope that the process begins and what is essentially you emerges. The block is a sign you're getting closer. Don't stop there. Fight to break through the wall like you are fighting for your life. Part of you is stuck on the other side."

Bernard

"BERNARD, WHAT MAKES you think your penis isn't big enough?" I probe gently. (Silently, I wonder how big is it? How presumptuous of me to assume it's all in his head. Truth is, he just may have a point, but I am in no position to get out my yardstick.)

"Well, I remember my father telling me I needed a splint for it. I remember he used to flash me with his. It was bigger, much bigger than mine," he recalls.

"But Bernard," I remind him, "your father was bigger, you were only a child then."

"Of course, you're right."

"What does your girlfriend think?" I ask.

"I don't know, she says she doesn't care, but I'm obsessed," he admits.

"What are you obsessed with?"

"How big they are, I mean her ex-boyfriends, I can't stop thinking about it."

"So what if their penises were bigger than yours, Bernard. Why do you care?"

"So what? So what? It kills me. It just kills me."

"What kills you, Bernard? Your girlfriend is telling you that she doesn't care and she's giving you no indication that she does. Bernard, do you realize that when we take her out of the equation what we're left with is a guy who's obsessed with other guys' penises? Is that what kills you?" (Nowhere has the art of subtraction been so well defined). Bernard grabs the side of the couch as my calculus reduces his torment to its source.

"Bernard, are you attracted to other men?" I notice his grip on the arm of my couch as I continue to explore his obsessive jealousy. His fingernails grow longer as I speak. Their impression is about to be forever preserved in Italian leather. Tacitly, I hold my breath. It's penetration I now fear however small his penis. It is not possible to bring this to his attention without traumatizing him for life. I want to jump out of my listening chair, I want to shout, "Hey, you want to talk about feelings, get this . . . how can I work while you're fucking up my couch?"

Instead, I maintain what's left of my composure.

"Are you using your girlfriend as a prophylactic? I mean, are you attracted to men vicariously through her? Bernard, are you jealous or are you homophobic?"

My oversimplification goes to the core and defies social grace. The hyperbole gets his attention. However effective, the therapeutic goal blurs as leather gives way to self-discovery. So much for the size of his penis, clearly his nails are long enough.

THE IRREGULARITY OF 14th Street and 9th Avenue draws you in like a dare to be different. By morning all the alcoholics have been swept aside with the used condoms and the empty liquor bottles. A neighborhood bum whose bedroom is this corner dances to music that no one else hears.

The only way to get into the corner building is to ring the intercom from the street and wait for someone to come down and open the elevator door. A huge *700* painted on the warehouse door shouts out from under a greasy shade of green, as though afraid of getting lost in this vortex of gender confusion. The geriatric pace of the elevator and the foul stench from the markets along the street cause most people to ring the bell strenuously, especially in the heat of summer.

Eventually, the elevator descends. One enters the rancid cubicle by violating gut instinct. A steel door slams against the frame with the metallic jolt of a car crash after the button's been pressed. Perversely, it remains motionless just long enough for it to be stuck. Then, reluctantly, it makes its way up and stops at Mel's. Mel's, a boutique on the second floor, is the only place in town where a guy can find a pair of patent leather heels in size 15.

After a shopping spree, Mel's customers usually hide what they have bought. On the way down, lace panties and silk bras are stuffed into an attaché case. Bulkier items like chiffon gowns usually get shoved in a red plastic bag with no logo and tucked under one arm.

Executives in pin stripes sweat a lot more than the drag queens. The fear of getting stuck is double jeopardy for those already prisoners of their own predilections. Tense executives position themselves at the door with hope and fear; approaching it with the reverence of the Wailing Wall they pray. The door jams anyway. During these moments malfunction is elevated to a state of holy terror. Feverishly, they fumble with the lock while trying to remain nonchalant. Gingerly, I intervene. I go out of my way to help. After I undo the quirky lock a partial "thank you" is muttered and the emancipated CEO races down the street incognito hailing the first cab. "Hey, it's OK" I think to myself, "I don't care how you dress. Have a nice day."

In order to build my practice I place my cards in Mel's, Bloomingdale's subdivision for the exceptionally "flexible" shopper. The cards sit on a pearlized counter. Snuggled next to ostrich feather scarves they pale against a variety of ads for sexual transgressions, indiscretions, and transfigurations. Nevertheless, some clients call.

Ronald

RONALD ENTERS TALL and handsome, an African American with all the accoutrements of a successful lawyer. His loose cashmere sweater gives the impression a black BMW is parked outside. Horn-rimmed glasses sit snugly on an aquiline slope setting off a well-developed intellect. A salt-and-pepper goatee contrasts nicely against his bald head.

Just going through a divorce, I assume. Before we begin he asks to use the bathroom. "Of course," I answer and direct him to the toilet without trying to be overly directive. Meanwhile, I wonder if it's been flushed. After a few minutes I thumb through my appointment book. I am up to next year when I wonder what's taking him so long? At last, I hear the bowl surge with contentment. Ronald has already begun letting go.

Suddenly he sits before me, radically transformed. A balding head rests on a female torso that is squeezed into a black dress with spaghetti straps that give way to the fullness of three crescent bulges, two on his chest. His ensemble is tastefully finished off with a Gucci bag and a pair of lizard heels. He is a chic seductress up to his neck. It's clear he got my card at Mel's.

"I can no longer bear living with a body that doesn't go with my head," he tells me. He bemoans the nature of his existence while the headless chicken from my childhood runs across the room in a wig.

PSYCHOTHERAPY IS AN unnatural profession. It requires a penetration that exceeds the intimacy between lovers with constraints that keep you strangers at the same time. I sit inside secrets. It's my day's work. Genetic males tell me they're women. I listen. Genetic females tell me they're men. I listen. Exhibitionists stick photos of their genitalia in my face. I see. Each secret is a scar, concealed to meet a standard of "normal" that no one identifies with but everyone aspires to. I am no exception.

> I AM A LES-BI-AN, a LESBIAN
> The syllables stick to the roof of my mouth.
> LESBIAN love of my life, light of my loins, my sin,
> my soul.
> LESBIAN. . . LES-BI-AN. The tip of my tongue,
> takes me three taps.
> LES-BI-AN . . . and still I have trouble saying it.

Why not a "woman's woman," a "lover of women," or just "gay?" It's quick, it's easy, it's compact, and it fits into sentences with just a fraction of the time. But "LES-BI-AN." The word is a showstopper. Tell someone you are one of those and you have changed their life forever.

Take my mother, for instance. I'd always looked like her. The similarity was striking. It was as if I wore her nose on my face and now she wanted it back with all her unborn grandchildren. Gladly, I would have returned the favor if at all possible. She called with a controlled anguish in her voice, anxious not to know the answer to the question she was about to ask: "Cloe, once you told me parents are like children. They only ask about what they're ready to deal with. Well, I'm asking . . ." I heard her breath take a phantom leap from the depths of her uterus. Venom surged from her womb as she asked the deadly question. "Are you a LES-BI-AN?" As she bore me, now suddenly, her life was in my hands. Guilt made me that owner. And, in a minute of silence we were pitted against each other, struggling for our own survival. If I live in truth she will die, I thought. My denial, my duplicity, my omission had been her life spring. Her unfulfilled fantasies, her future grandchildren depended on me. In that one minute I thrashed against the walls like a captured animal while she waited silently. I struggled endlessly. Then, in submission and in courage I answered. "Yes, I'm a LES-BIAN." The dead silence that followed halted the flow of a thousand generations. Only their shrouds would remain on earth and I was to blame. I held the motherless cord in my hand while the ghost on the other end forgot who I was for many long and bitter months. For a second time, I was hurled into the world but from a chilled and wrenching womb.

WOMEN CRY AT weddings . . . for all that was, for all that will never be again. But for me it is different. I am different.

A glass penthouse commissioned for a holy ceremony overlooks Central Park from a charmed position. It pierces the bellies of swollen clouds and dwarfs the height of skyscrapers. Penguins carry silver trays anointed by the Pope. I dance with several men, occasionally stepping on their feet. It's clear I'm not used to being led. Thanks to the kindness of strangers it appears to go unnoticed. Finally, the time has come.

Amelia dictates that we take our places. I am left with no place. On or off the line . . . either choice is a lie, but which one is closer to the truth? No choice leaves me standing with the married women. Suddenly, it's silent. You can hear the clocks ticking, like the hearts of unborn babies in the bellies of so many mothers meant to be—each woman for herself by herself.

Reluctantly, I take a place with the unmarried women. Deliberately, I stand behind the others against the wall. Surely, I think to myself, I won't ruin anyone else's chances this way. The loneliest push and pull, vying for the best position, trying to anticipate the path of this tender missile with a secret desperation that has already bored holes in their hearts. I just stand there, numbed by a time that has passed me by.

At first, she teases us with the coveted torch. Carelessly, she wastes time joking about who is next. Thoughtlessly, she waves the bouquet without throwing it.

"Who wants it?" She peddles her power. We laugh, but a launch at Cape Canaveral could not be more serious. She hurls the prize into the air with great zest. The generosity is so exuberant it hits the back wall where I'm standing and the bouquet lands in my arms. I am stunned. In a flash, I can see the widened eyes of a dozen Cinderellas facing me with their loss. I hold the soft petals hard to my chest, so hard I'm crushing them. I have never won anything before.

But, just as kids and a husband take root in my breast, a white blur rushes toward me flailing her arms, shouting frantically, "I didn't mean to throw it so hard. Do-over. Do-over!" Amelia tries to grab the bouquet from me. I resist.

"Amelia," I cry, "I caught it, it's mine." I can hear the echo of my own words in the hush of the circling crowd. Ashamed to show how real the game now seems, I cradle the bouquet for a minute longer before she rips the dream ot of my heart.

Our quarrel is over with one sharp pull. She regains her posture and steps to the center of the floor. In a determined voice she resumes her casting position. "We're doing it over, everyone get back in line!" The players whisper to each other with renewed excitement. Exalted by their second chance, they line up with furious discipline, adjusting eyes and posture to the slightest nuances of Amelia's right arm. As she waves her wand, I slip away hating her.

"Do-over?" That was an expression we would shout twenty years ago when we played handball, defending our rights to that concrete slab in the back of the school yard till it was time to go home for supper. We had spent most of our childhood facing that stern monolith; returning its answers with another. We knew its cracks and bumps the way you know your lover's back. That perpendicular structure was our corner of the world. "Do-overs" were part of the rules then. It was a last chance to win . . . not lose.

A lesbian, once a whore, then a madam, finally a

bride; at last her life was on track . . . but not her flowers. Now she was a fashion designer marrying a prominent New York financier—how important that her flowers be re-routed. I don't know how I got home that day. I think I took a cab. It was raining—or was I crying so hard? I do remember passing through the screaming reds and oranges of 42nd Street as if I was smashing through blotches painted by someone who hated colors. The impact hurt for a moment, and then there was nothing on the other side.

Willie

"IT'S NOTHING, DOC. It's nothing. I mean, I've never told anyone this before. I am afraid you'll hold it against me. I know ya will."

"Try to trust me with it, Willie."

"It's hard, Dr. Goldwin but . . ."

"What is it, Willie?"

"Well, I grew up on a mental ward, Six South. My home was a psychiatric hospital in South Central, LA till I was eighteen. My parents' faces changed with the shifts. My brothers and sisters were all throwaway kids like myself. When I was released last year, I told people I grew up on a psycho unit like it was normal. But people would treat me differently then, like I was dirty or somethin'. After a while the question 'Where'd ya grow up?' would put me in a tailspin. Not cause I'm ashamed or nothin' but 'cause I could tell it made them forget what they were gonna ask next. So I started telling a little white lie, sorta speak. Like, I grew up in a large complex in South Central, 'near' that psychiatric hospital on Ocean Avenue."

"I see. And how are you doing now?"

"Well, I still have some problems."

"Like what?"

"Nothing serious . . . Well, I'm left-handed but I eat with my right hand because the food tastes better that way. What do ya think? I mean, I can't read the front of your mind but if you turn around I can read the back of it through the center. But even then I can't tell. How many sheep do I need to buy a wife, Dr. Goldwin?"

IN MOMENTS OF angst I seek out the curvaceous ear of my old friend Annie. We know each other from a short story that never ended. To her my life is a series of convoluted misadventures, perhaps poetic but only from a distance. In turn, she is a monument of domesticity at its best, however politically correct. She lives inside the Statue of Liberty, the libidinous libertarian who stands for the freedom of others because she doesn't know how to swim herself. Also a therapist, she would prefer to ride the waves, but is afraid to get wet. Another shrink stuck in a bad marriage. As a result, I always know where to find her when I need to talk and we talk often. With torch in hand, she is my guiding light. Of all the details of my homosexual eroticisms I do tell. From the way our words have fallen our relationship is strictly platonic but she listens with prurient interest. Laden with the broken bones of my broken stories, she is well-versed in the series of false starts I call my love affairs. We soften our good-byes with plans to meet.

Then one day, with a sudden tug, she pulls herself out of the mud of suburbia and swims to shore. She arrives at my door on a Saturday night, and for the first three nights that follow she does not speak, she does not eat. She takes her bloodshot eyes out of her head and glues them to the corner window that oversees 14th Street. She is transfixed by the circus below. There are no enticements strong enough to detach her stare from the glass. Feathered glowing transmutants, she is under their spell, intoxicated by their glorious irreverence.

It is not a new occurrence. It has happened before. In fact, a warning in my lease reads: *Beware of the intoxicating view. If you charge guests a fee—ten percent of that fee will be deducted from your security*

deposit. The failure to report any such revenue is a vio-
lation of the lease and will result in eviction. Of course,
you will also be held responsible for the landlord's legal
fees incurred in litigation.

When she does come to, she is emancipated. In the spirit of liberty she places herself on my mound and rides me through the night. When she arrives at her destination she yells, "*chacun à son goût,*" and unpacks her bags. Manhattan is her town now although, after two years, she is still battling with her husband over who gets what and why.

We are not "just" friends, we are the best of friends. There is nothing we can't say to each other. We revel in slurring each other as a form of etiquette.

Annie calls in between clients. "Good morning, slut. How are you? Want to meet for a cappuccino?"

"OK pancake breasts. How's an hour from now— Dean and Deluca?"

"Make that two hours, monkey buttons. I have one more head to shrink." When we get together we laugh about our tryst. "I'll try anything once, you know. But I am forever heterosexual," she reminds me, she reminds herself.

"You can't catch lesbianism," I comfort her, "unless you already have it."

I WAS AT the movies with an old friend Paul when the effects of my isolation became glaringly apparent. He offered me some buttered popcorn as a nun blew a kiss to a dead man walking. Lost in the scene, I placed my greasy hand ever so gently on the top of his head. With my eyes glued to the super screen I used a soft petting motion, ordinarily reserved for my dog, to express my gratitude. Engrossed in the film, the short stubby texture of his balding head was indistinguishable from the short hairs of Sigmund, my Weimaraner. "Good dog, good dog," I blurted out. The words fell from my mouth like bricks when I wasn't looking. Dark wasn't dark enough. Sinking to the bottom of my seat dead man walking was executed to the sound of wild dog barking.

It was all too clear. The pressures of life were caving in on me since I returned from Stolen Ridge in Southern California. Annie was mysteriously missing, maybe dead. I was not relating normally. I watched the credits roll down the screen through translucent memories. I was experiencing life through those memories. They were making a double exposure out of everything.

My story had started long before I realized. There had been a bizarre murder in my laundry room when I lived on Perry Street. Greta, a neighbor from the sixth floor, did her laundry late one night. According to the police she carried her laundry bag and a box of Tide into the gray concrete room like she had many times before. She and I had spent hours in that room sharing our dirty laundry. We were about the same age. After stuffing her soiled clothes into the washing machine she took a seat on a vibrating wooden bench.

Greta was an antenna turned upside down. She hated to be alone down there. I know she was frightened that night. Bored by the multicolored swirls she picked up a psychology journal lying on the bench. It was a journal I had just left behind. It had no flashy pictures, no sexy articles. *The Journal of Abnormal Psychology* is too sick to be sexy. After thumbing through a few pages she switched it for a soggy copy of *Playgirl* magazine lying on the floor. The discharge from an overflowing washer softened the cover and felt like mush in her hands but she would take Brad Pitt's body anyway she could get it.

We used to talk about our fantasies. Greta liked to dream about being beautiful. The machines' constant rhythm relaxed her into believing she was beautiful, as beautiful as the stars. Thumbing through their dreamy lives helped her ignore a gnawing fear that she was in some kind of danger.

Suddenly, the churning cylinders muffled heavy breathing from behind. Wheezing like a wounded animal, he emerged out of a mechanical symphony of washers and dryers. Greta shivered in concert with the convulsive sounds that drew near. The hunger was at her neck... Biting into a rapid pulse heightened his own. Ripping into her breasts smothered him red, bringing him to a warm thick high . . . It was all over before the wash was done.

Neatly, he wrapped the parts he had a taste for, mainly the breasts and the buttocks, in T-shirts that were still warm with the smell of Tide. Meticulously, he placed them in the laundry bag. The police were able to determine that much. She was a takeout dinner, except for her head, which, severed from her neck, was left behind to swirl a crimson shade of bubbles with the rest of her body.

The case was never solved. All the tenants in the building were questioned but there were no suspects. The killer left no leads. The police were stumped. It was the perfect crime.

THE DAY AFTER Greta's murder I had had a job interview. It was the final inquest. I'd had over six interviews in the past two months for a prestigious consulting firm in Rockefeller Plaza. I had been tested and re-tested, evaluated, and assessed each time by a different gentleman of proper descent, each a psychological consultant. My thermometer had been taken and re-taken. The national firm was a tribe of medicine men, Ph.D.'s who provided hot chicken soup in the form of psychotherapy to ailing corporate presidents. I was to be the first medicine woman on the roster. It was in the bag I was told. We shook hands on it. By the second year I would be making over $100,000. I only had to meet the head psychologist, boss of bosses, and I would be on my way to the top. It was just protocol I was told.

Like the others he had silver hair and thin lips. He wore suspenders and a belt, which made me wonder what he was hiding. But I could deal with it. I was going to be the first woman, first Jew in the New York office. Groundbreaking, I thought to myself. How Mississippi. He greeted me with aplomb as he took a seat next to me rather than on the other side of the big oak desk. That relaxed me. "Cloe, I'm so glad to meet you," he said warmly. I had no reason to doubt it. Then, he took a big breath. "Watch out, watch out," I told myself in visceral code.

"Cloe, what I am about to say isn't easy. I am sorry, truly sorry—but there's been a mistake." I was frozen in my chair so comfortable. "The director has made a mistake. I can't let him hire you," he told me plainly with the same aplomb he used to greet me.

"Why?" Now dead, I asked him to shoot me. "Why?" I asked, about to plunge a dagger through his heart.   He took time to reword his thoughts while I attempted to administer artificial resuscitation to myself with false hope. Somewhere it's tomorrow.

"Cloe," he dared to call me by my first name again, "you're just not right for the position."

"I don't understand, Dr. Kevorkian, I don't want to die just yet," I said quietly to myself. "I was right for the position last week. What's happened between now and then?"

"Cloe, you'd be advising presidents of Fortune 500 companies. Most of them are racist, anti-Semite Wasps like myself," is what I hear. "You understand, Cloe," he starts again, as if that were not enough, "you're just too creative for the job.   It's clear from your interviews, from the results of your tests."

"Too creative," I repeated the phrase over and over again, to Annie, to Paul, to my mother, to anyone who would listen to how I had been wronged . . . and then I bought my first canvas. I'll show those bastards "too creative" I said to myself as I stood on line at Pearl Paint, an art store on Canal Street. Each tube of paint and each brush I charged catapulted me into a new dimension. That dimension was a boundless field of white. The slightest gesture of my wrist unleashed me. Lost in the spirit of the line there was nothing but to paint. I had discovered a new dimension. I should have sued the firm, but they went bankrupt.

Anyway, I was in love . . . with the smell of paint.

. . . THEN THERE WAS the invisible man who lived downstairs. His name was Gordon Hartcourt. You don't always know who your neighbors are in Manhattan, even if your floor is their ceiling. At first the calls were sporadic; decent if not cordial requests to stop. "Your fumes are permeating our boundaries," he complained. "You are asphyxiating me. Please stop." I breathed to paint while Gordon panted to breathe. We were inextricably linked. Inhalation versus inspiration. Both just causes however diametrically opposed. I could not stop. As I threw myself into each new painting his requests escalated into a tirade of unmentionable exercises in self-expression. Initially, it was unnerving. The haunting, faceless voice began as soon as my feet hit the floor, as if I was stepping in shit. "You are destroying me. I cannot sleep. I cannot eat. I cannot work and it is your fault. I will get you for this," he warned, "and for the occasional howls of love unmitigated by an insufficiently thick carpet." We spoke as often as lovers did with the same intensity, at all hours of the day and night. Two, three in the morning was not unusual.

The conversations, always by phone, far exceeded the peevishness over the smell of paint. Each of us had become a dumping ground for the other, housebound recipients for all that had gone wrong with the day. Secretly, I had become attached to this peculiar freedom. I looked forward to it. In no way did our anger threaten our relationship. We could call each other anything at anytime. It was a twisted sort of unconditional regard based on rent control. One does not give up a cheap apartment in Manhattan easily.

THEN IT WAS spring. Pointing with an arthritic bent, the way an old friend waves a shaky forefinger, the tree limb directly in front of my brownstone pushed against an open door. Arched, from across the sidewalk she entered my studio apartment like an unwanted guest I secretly desired. I dare not cut it. It would be an act against nature. The old tree had its roots on Perry Street long before the concrete foundation of the building was cast. Like an American Indian it staked its claim first and I was bound to its position.

It was me, my dog, the canvases, and paint everywhere on everything. Then there was my mother. It was a chilly winter morning. I thought I heard a knock at the door. Usually, she would let me know when she was coming to visit. Then, an hour or two later I would hear my name from down the street. "Cloe," she would sing after taking the E-train from Kew Gardens to the Village. This morning there was one knock. I opened the door that opened directly to the street. There stood an old gray woman twisted in pain. She knew my name. She limped inside like she had never been young. "I was on my way to work, but I can't make it," she said. "I need a doctor—I don't know if I'm going to make it."

My mother was forever. Every morning like this morning she took the train to work for one decade, then another. Who was this woman who presumed to know me? Anyway, Jewish mothers never die. They give too much to live, so how can they die?

Frantically, I called God—one specializing in gastroenterology. After many calls I discovered he and his colleagues were at a medical convention in Los Angeles. Finally I located one who had remained behind. That made me worry, but I was desperate.

Convinced it was an emergency, he summoned us to his office somewhere uptown in between life and death. We took the first cab we could get. After putting his ear to her belly he ordered her to drink a gallon of liquid soap for an omniscient eye to follow. She was still well enough to complain about the bitter taste of liquid fortune.

Then the wait . . . Finally he called. "Don't panic but your mother has a time bomb in her intestines that is about to rupture. If it does, it will kill her. Get her to the hospital now. We'll cut her up in the morning and, if she lives, she won't be the same—but stay calm. It will be all right. She has to go sooner or later anyway."

My mother left the hospital repaired but not restored. She made my couch her bed for the rest of her life. Many times we fought over it. "Mom, it's not comfortable. It's not large enough. It doesn't have enough cushioning. The leather is cold. It's cracking. It's OK to sit on, but not to die on." I begged her to let me sleep on it. I demanded she take my bed instead, but she refused. She needed to feel she was sacrificing something for me even then, so I gave her that.

Quietly, I would awake from the shadows to paint in between the couch and the easel while she slept. I entered a boundless space through a canvas curtain. Gravity no longer applied. It was where I would go. There was nowhere else. The studio was about twelve by twenty feet.

Hours later, my mother would awake from behind the black bars falling across her face. With no words for her pain, "good morning" was a lie. Silently she would get up to go to the bathroom, pour herself a cup of black coffee already thick from the early morning, and sit at the edge of my bed directly in front of the easel. "Wait, let me put my glasses on and see what you've done." Her enthusiasm left no time for "good morning." She followed each stroke with a curiosity meant for an unfinished mystery. How faithful she was.

At the same time, she hadn't helped me through my doctorate for me to become a starving artist. She accepted my struggle the way one accepts the genetic anomaly of their offspring—not without some form of responsibility. I was, after all, her daughter who painted without really knowing why she didn't dance instead. After a few sips of coffee, she regained her keen sensibility and her critical power. I was living out the creative fantasy she would not allow herself. She was the artist I became. Now, her responsibility was to tell me what she thought. I could take her advice or leave it. That was the understanding. She looked at the section I was working on. "Sure you mean that? It just doesn't look honest," she would say. Sometimes I experimented with her suggestions on the spot and was grateful. Other times she annoyed the hell out of me. Then, as a last resort, I would wait until she left the room before I tried them out. Of course, she would come back from the bathroom, immediately notice the change on her way to the couch and glow. "There you go, Cloe. Now you've got it."

Other times she was more vociferous. "Cloe, you're off. It doesn't work." The symbiosis would rupture. I felt like killing her but she was already dying. We were on the edge of the world in a small box. There was no escape. She left me no choice but to threaten cremation. Sternly, she reminded me it was against the Jewish religion. She knew I was an atheist. She didn't hold it against me but insisted on a proper Jewish burial for herself. "Ashes to ashes," I would respond as she lit up another cigarette. Time decreased the bargaining power of my threat until I would have no leverage. Neither of us would win the game.

"How about dinner?" usually worked. We threw on our coats. Sung Tieng, a Chinese restaurant, was just down the street. Together we would feast on the simple pleasures of wonton soup, followed by shrimp in lobster sauce. Then, after a few months, she stopped opening her fortune cookies. It was time to order in.

Still, there was one fight we had religiously just before we went to sleep. It started something like, "You know, Cloe, your dog Sigmund isn't too bright. I mean, I've been noticing he's just not as bright as Lulu was... remember Lulu, Cloe?" Of course, I thought to myself, with one eye still closed. I came home from school one day and found a crowd of kids standing in front of my house. I made my way in between them. My mother held a tiny puppy with scraggly gray curls in her arms. "Wow," I said. "She's so tiny, looks like she was just born." I had given up the hope of ever getting a dog, even though I would wish for one on the way to school every day. "Would you like a dog like this?" she asked. My mouth made way for the word "sure," as she handed me the leash. How well I remembered Lulu. She was a toy poodle the family drove crazy with too many kisses.

But then a competitive edge to the conversation would get to me. From her corner of the couch she whispered loud enough to wake me, "Cloe, are you still up?"

"Yea," I lied. Frequently, the phone would ring at around this time. Assuming it was my neighbor I didn't always answer. Especially, if a feud was about to break out on the home front.

"Cloe, remember Lulu's discipline, how she would hold it in on the weekends and let the family sleep? Sigmund never does that, Cloe. How come?"

"What do you have against Sigmund?" I would ask but she just went on.

"You know, Cloe, Glue would have been a better name than Sigmund . . . he's just so clingy, how smart can he be?"

"Why do you do this, Mom?" I asked half asleep. "Why do you always compare the two dogs? Sigmund's dependency needs have nothing to do with his intelligence," assuming a professional posture now that I was up. "Anyway, Sigmund is a pointer; Lulu was just another pretty face." This conversation would continue until, at some point, the repetition became funny.

As usual, she described Lulu's superior qualities, neglecting the dog's profound neurosis. "Lulu understood every word, Cloe. Nothing got by her." She recalled her Lulu with the affection of a child, which endeared her to me. But then she would start again about Sigmund. "You know, he never stops staring at you. He even follows you to the bathroom. If you're gonna be in a co-dependent relationship, why not choose a man?"

"You forget Mom I'm gay." How conveniently reality fades when the lights are off.

She would continue. "Sigmund doesn't even eat like a normal dog. The way he takes his food out of the bowl and drops it in front of you, wherever you are, just so he can stare at you while he eats. It's sick Cloe, it's sick. My own husband wasn't so devoted."

"Mom, it's how he eats all of his meals. Why not just accept it. Yes, his loyalty is excessive—but it's the breed."

Then she would remind me, "Lulu had her own life—at least she kept her food in the bowl. She was an independent dog."

Secretly, I wondered if Sigmund and I had violated the boundaries between woman and beast. "Can we make it?" We would ask ourselves this question every morning as we raced to the street. Relieved when the pale yellow stream hit the pavement with the force of a horse . . . the vicarious satisfaction was undeniable. When neighbors object to the residual browning effect on the sidewalk we don't get defensive like other dogs. "It's an antique finish. It does no harm," is the retort. "Did you know prisoners in the concentration camps would urinate on their own wounds to prevent infection? It's an anti-bacterial agent." After a minute or two Sigmund reposi-tions himself . . . this time in the gutter. The crescendo builds slowly as his hind legs arch. With a wider spread, after some consideration, the denouement . . . a crude log hits the road, then another. Renewed at last. Free to go back home. Were we embroiled in a symbiotic relation-ship? We didn't think so.

"Imagine," she asked, "Where would you be today if I brought you up like Sigmund."

Still living with my mother, I guess—was my answer. Then, as if that were not enough, I let her have it. "Mom, did you forget how the ASPCA came to our house and threatened to take Lulu away for biting kids in the neighborhood?"

She would come back at me even stronger. "He's a German dog, isn't he, Cloe? I heard Hitler genetically engineered the Weimaraner, didn't he?"

Lulu was her baby. "Don't you know," she would say, "dogs are the closest things we have to angels." Lulu could do no wrong. She finished everything on her plate. She never dared grow up. And, she listened—unlike her daughter. But it wasn't about that. My mother's life had shrunk to the size of the room we lived in. *Lulu and Sigmund* was a tune she would hum the way you sing an old song you've sung a thousand times before. It still sounds good.

GRETA'S KILLER HAD not been found. Her ghost haunted the building looking for him. And my mother's death was just around the corner. Death was everywhere. But the fear of death can go either way. It can motivate you or immobilize you, depending on how you see it.

I unfurled the covers one morning after my fatal job interview like shedding a skin with nothing to lose. I saw a line on a subway poster. It went something like: "Life is short but if you do it right once it is long enough." This underground philosophy would be my driving force.

Canvases leaned against the walls, framing our lives while my mother slept. Slowly, the cancer was traveling to her brain. It was six months since I had started painting. By now I had twenty slides of twenty paintings. I could hear her moan in her sleep as I proceeded to label them, jamming the basics around the narrow margins, including the painting's name, size and date.

I left the apartment that day like crawling out of a shell that suddenly had gotten too small. Halfway down Bleecker Street I realized I had forgotten to put my name on the slides. After tiptoeing back into the apartment for a pen, I was ready. Down Bleecker Street again, right on LaGuardia Place, across Houston to Soho. With a deep breath I would jump at the chance to take my work seriously.

I entered the first gallery I came to on South Broadway. A woman behind a wrought-iron desk imparted a hard-edged beauty to the abstract paintings, her blonde hair pulled back in a French twist. Frequently, galleries use beautiful women to provide context. Intimidated by the straightness of her nose, I asked more humbly than is really me, "Do you accept slides?" The porcelain figure answered. "It takes six months for slides to be reviewed." Winter fell from her tongue.

Suddenly, the season changed. A man approached the desk with the casual confidence of the owner. I repeated my question as if for the first time, shoving my slides into his hands. Reluctantly, he accepted the plastic sheet, making the woman behind the desk angry rather than cold. Turning to the window, he raised the twenty images to the light outside, leaving me to stare at the back of his head. When he turned around it was with a smile. "YES!" he said. "Yes!" he said twice.

There was no reason to walk home when I could fly. My mother was still sleeping when I returned. I placed the signed contract over her eyes, balancing it on her nose. Gripped by tender joy she read the tiny print the way the Ten Commandments ought to be read. She rose feet above the floor to dance with me. She was too sick to get up. I would like to say the story ends here. I would like to say I went on to become a rich and famous artist . . .

INSTEAD, I FOUND a part-time job in a clinic uptown. I could pay the rent with time left over to paint. It was my first day. The director was filling me in. "Give each client a full session. When you're finished with his head, escort him down the hall to get his nuts and bolts adjusted. The surrogate assigned to his case will get back to you with a detailed report on his performance." It was the Advanced Center for Sexual Adversities. The director of the clinic handed me the roster with utmost care. Confidentiality is paramount in this business. I slipped the list under my arm, checking off clients as I saw them. Tales of woe, crucial contexts of projectiles crushing their owners in the fall.

A Wall Street analyst, a mortician, a cello player . . . All kinds of men fail to rise to the occasion. The day was moving along quite smoothly. I glanced at the roster for my last client. At first I was struck by a coincidence. My last client had the same name as my downstairs neighbor, Gordon Hartcourt at 48 Perry Street. It was clear our paths had crossed again. Diagnoses: PREMATURE EJACULATION. With both legs up on my desk and a cup of coffee in hand the victim of my fantasies sat directly in front of me while he sat so tensely in the waiting room. Now, for the visit of a lifetime, Gordon Hartcourt.

He enters with his tail between his legs. He does not recognize me, I assume. We have never met in person. The session proceeds as usual. Silently, meticulously, I collect the gory details of his crippled sex life. No surprise to me, I think. My heart pounds for the denouement. The evidence is mounting. He is offended by the smell of women (especially, the one that lives above him.) He prefers the bottom to the top (that I already know). "Can you help me with my problem?" He asks, he begs. "You bet I can," I think to myself. Caught off guard, he asks my full name. I oblige with a card. A head-on collision occurs. He finds his voice an octave higher. "I thought you were a painter," he says weakened at the knees . . . Now, fully emasculated, he is cured of premature ejaculation.

"Let's make a deal." I grasp the opportunity, forsaking psychology for art. "Let me paint in peace and— The director halts my fantasy with one swift knock, then another. "Your client is waiting, Dr. Goldwin. Shall I get him for you?"

The rules are hard and fast according to the American Psychological Association. Ethical constraints prevail. The best interest of the client must be preserved. However tempted, the opportunity to humiliate a client and bring them to their knees is forbidden, even if therapeutic to the therapist. The director knocks again. "Are you there, Dr. Goldwin?"

"Dr. Trueblood, I would like to see him, really I would . . . but I can't. We're neighbors."

Over the months that followed he continued to call, much the same as always. The smell of paint—just a springboard to rail against. But the conversations were different now. The utter humiliation I subjected him to and then saved him from engendered a kind of affection. I had one up on him. Now, his calls humored me.

CALVARY HOSPICE IS located in the Bronx somewhere between death and dying.   Mona Lisa look-alikes, replete with peace and understanding, frequent the halls, draped in bat black.   It's clear from their solemn show of kindness that they are members of a secret sorority of high distinction.   Complete with this understanding, I inquire where my mother's room is.   Follow the narrow hall to the end, I am told.   I do so piously, humbled by the ghostly silence.   There is no rushing in and out of rooms as in other hospitals. There was no pain. It was beyond that.   Within two months everyone in the building would be dead except for the fleeting movements of the staff.   A handful of doctors help the dead die.   At Calvary the physician's power was no more than the orderly's.

My mother, half-paralyzed, raises a heavy weight— her arm.   She sings when I come in, "Look everyone. This is my daughter, my beautiful daughter."   I am the silver dot that glistens in the center of her cornea. She greets me with smiling lips tilted upward toward the way I am. I rush to kiss her face.   Each day she is a little worse.   I have Marino ices, five different flavors. More than she will ever eat.   It is the only thing she can get down.

"How are you, mom?"   I ask as I pull the paper off a small wooden spoon and feed her the way she once fed me.   "Which flavor would you like to try first?"

She says, "Strawberry."   It is the only decision she has made all day.   There has been a month of days just like this one.

The nurse enters the room without knocking.   There are no secrets here.   "How are ya Lotte?   See ya got your ices," she says, "I'll be back in a minute."

She returns with a steel lift to hoist my mother out of the bed. "No, you've got to help her. We can help her together," I plead to the nurse. "It's too early. Mom, you can go on your own. Tell her you can. Mom?" She answers with no answer.

Instead, the nurse speaks for her. "Ma'am, we can't change her diapers otherwise." I didn't know she was wearing diapers. She had kept it from me.

It's not long now. A tidal wave builds in my chest. She made me promise not to ask her to hold on. I no longer joke about cremating her. That was when she could still laugh. Instead, I ask " A cup of water, more ices, maybe? How about the lemon, mom?"

She motions that I bring my head close to hers. "My only regret," she whispers in my ear, "is that in your life you won't have the kind of daughter I have had in mine."

I leave to get a cup of coffee and when I return the nurse calls me over to the main desk. "Your mother has expired." Expired? No. Library cards expire, not mothers, not my mother. "Mom," I yell in a whisper. "Mom . . ." I bleed tears. She is still white with no answer.

When I return home my one-room apartment is too big with the couch so empty. I decide to move . . .

13

WITH NOTHING LEFT to lose I packed up my life. With all that was mine . . . dog, paints and brushes I drove cross-country in my old MG. Destination: West, my convertible top down all the way.

After three days and three nights, I stopped at one of those chain restaurants off the highway, somewhere across the plains where potatoes grew like flowers. I got on line for an iced coffee with a roll and butter. I had been driving all night, but I was awake enough to notice what looked like a funny nurse's hat on top of the waitress's head. For a minute I wondered if she was my mother's nurse. I couldn't believe my mother was dead. If I didn't remind myself of the reality, it would jolt me from behind when I wasn't paying attention.

"S'cuse me ma'am, did you say iced coffee?"

"Yes, an iced coffee, please."

"What's that?" she said.

I asked myself if she was joking, but from the length of time she held her hand to her chin I realized she wasn't. The ingredients had always seemed self-evident. I explained them anyway. While she was looking for the ice, I sought the reassurance of a stranger. "Do you believe it, she doesn't know what iced coffee is?" I commented to the man on line behind me.

An awkward silence followed. "Sounds like a good idea to me!"

Was I on *Candid Camera* or in the *Twilight Zone*? Here, I was the strange one, my arrogance a New York state of mind. Finally, the woman with the funny nurse's hat returned with a smile. Eager to see what I thought, she handed me the secret potion with both hands. Too rushed to wrestle with the plastic top I thanked her profusely halfway out the door. It was no surprise . . . three little ice cubes sinking in a sickly beige solution. The ticket I got for speeding onto the highway ramp was no surprise either.

Six days later we arrived. Mountains replaced sky-scrapers imprinted on burnt-out corneas. Round and round the mountains with strawberry fields sandwiched in between lifted me to the promise of a new beginning. Slopes of green carpet cradled the road into town.

Before all else, I had to find a pharmacy. Ads for Revo glasses and Birkenstock sandals made it clear. They knew what iced coffee was here. Spotting one in the center of this all-too-perfect town, I opened the glass door, jingling the bells above it.

"Good morning. How are you today? How's the dog?" The woman behind the counter greeted me as if we were old friends, each word ending on a high note. I looked again but didn't recognize her.

Trying to replicate the same cheer the way one rehearses new lines for a play I responded awkwardly. "Uh, fine, thank you . . . and yourself?"

"Just as good as can be. How can I help you, dear?" She asked with a smile that made me want to hug her.

"Well," I said in an octave lower, "I need some Tampax."

She handed me the super-absorbent box, as if she knew me intimately. Then she asked a question that struck a deep chord. "Would you like to use the bath-room?"

I was paralytic with disbelief; her kindness was more than I could bear. At no time, in no place, had any-one ever offered their bathroom after buying a box of Tampax. Not in New York, not in Paris, not in Jerusalem. And how often I asked, "Can I use your bathroom, please?" Only to be rejected, vilified by the mere request.

My mind was made up. Regardless of whether I had died in a swift car crash I had no recollection of and had landed in heaven, or had actually reached a place here on earth, I was staying! It was Stolen Ridge in Southern California.

The streets of Stolen were framed in lush mountains with a sea that frothed at its border. There were no fat or ugly people. Most were blonde, healthy types dressed in beach clothes unencumbered by style. Minorities were sorely missing. I began to suspect a secret underground that housed the fringe against their will. Perhaps a concentration camp that I myself would soon be sent to. Gingerly, I walked the streets careful not to dirty anything.

Suddenly, Aunt Ceil flashed her big face at me. Her white teeth turned yellow as she came at me from a small hole in the sidewalk. Aunt Ceil wasn't like other seals I had seen on TV when I was a kid. She scared me. I had no words for the fishy smell of lox on her breath. Casually, she picked me up. Caustically, she brushed the gray, straggly hairs on her chin across my face. Those hairs terrorized me. Now, forty years later slowly, imperceptibly, those same hairs grow out of my chin. Now as then they still scare me (I hope no one notices them).

I DIDN'T KNOW anyone in California except Patricia. She lived on a houseboat that contemplated travel but never went anywhere. While I was visiting, the boat jerked forward and I cut my finger on a sharp knife. My pinkie hung like it didn't belong to the rest of my hand. Frightened by the amount of blood rushing to mix with the salad dressing I yelled for help. "Patricia, I need to get to an emergency room, I can't stop the bleeding." Intentionally, she offered no assistance. She refused to give me directions, to even let me use the phone. Instead, she wanted me to pray the pain would stop. Let her pray, I thought to myself, I need a doctor. The rage made me bleed harder. Patricia was a Christian Scientist. Eventually the bleeding stopped, as did our friendship.

She tried to convince me that if I hurt myself again she would help. Waving her healing powers across my face, she showed off a blue light emanating from her fingertips. My inability to see her gift widened the gap between us. At a loss for words, to bridge the gap we decided to go to an art opening in town.

Openings were wakes in the early 1990s. Dressed in reverential black, everyone stood around remarking how great the work looked. The art market was dead and the coffin was open. No one was buying. Not in New York. Not in California. The viewing was at a chic gallery on the outskirts of town. I entered swallowing the experience whole. From a distance I noticed several cardboard forms, cutouts of men and women clamped and bolted onto each other, suspended from the ceiling with the same ropes that framed them. Their size commanded attention.

Grateful my pinkie was still attached to my hand I

picked at the hors d'oeuvre tray.   Serendipitous thoughts circled my mind as I found myself standing behind a fire-red mane starting high above the heads of others.   Shiny silk strands passed over the woman's shoulders down to her hips. The length of her hair led me to believe she did not like change in her life. Curious for the Amazon's head to swivel, I waited for the other side of the moon to reveal itself.

A simple turn of the head jarred my expectations. "Hi, I'm Montana. Are you new in town? I've never seen you before." She was a stunning contradiction to my expectations. Her sinuous structure made sense. It was a massive pedestal for green fields in her eyes, underlined by an open smile, emphasized by the comma in her chin. I pulled myself out of her expanse to answer. Eager to assert a ready-made connection I disregarded her question. "Look, your gold necklace is the same as my bracelet! They go together."

She imposed her beauty on me with an invitation I could not refuse. "Let's get together sometime. Give me a call," she said.

In my twenties I had been busy making patterns I can no longer deny in my forties. I have, to my own demise, an undeniable attraction to ostensibly heterosexual women. It's not deliberate. It's not even conscious. I am wired to know women who yearn for other women, however suppressed their desire. I am a radar dish. She smiled a smile that beget another smile, and I took her card. It indicated she was the artist.

I have a habit of buying shoes that do not fit. It doesn't matter if they are on sale or full price. Obsessive-compulsive, impulsive, regardless, when a pair of shoes catches my eye I must have them. It doesn't matter if they don't fit. It doesn't matter if I can't afford them. If they are my size, they should fit and they will.   Inevitably, the pinch becomes the blister that breaks my heart.

The simple fact is that you will never know anyone better than when you first meet them. It's only then that you see them objectively, for who they are, not for who you need them to be. I ignore this paradox, this interpersonal imperative. I snip off truths from awareness as if I was hemming a dress. I tailor my perceptions to my needs, eschewing unwanted material in the service of my ideal love. These truths that rub me the wrong way are the ones that hemorrhage later. The gut knows what the brain doesn't have the stomach to accept. It's smarter that way.

PENDULOUS ... TO JUST breathe and paint between the
sea and the sky, the horizon was my new home. From
my house on top of a canyon, from the supermarket, I
could hear the ocean roar. It followed me everywhere
like a faithful friend. I had, by chance, stumbled onto a
new beginning. I was living inside a dream. Pulsating
with life, thankful for each sweet breath lightly salted by
the sea, I called Montana.

"Hi, Montana. Remember me? It's Cloe." Tender
tortured romance, how new. How old. Pattern of patterns. "We met at your opening? I was wondering if
you felt like getting together?" The softness of her
voice eases me into myself. We know each other and
now we will discover how. This evening? Did she say
this evening? Stolen Ridge love friend, come now,
come this instant. "Great then," I answered with a stud-
ied unstudied tone. "I'll see you at my place at 8:00
p.m." I hung up grateful to be alive.

... Motherless. I am a motherless child, I thought
to myself, as I cut tomatoes for a salad. Montana was
late. My father died when he was still alive. We were
never close. I mourned the loss of him during my childhood. But how I missed the sound of my mother's
voice. How I wished I could pick up the phone and talk
to her about small things, a sale, a good movie, how to
roast a turkey. The singular responsibility of my own
existence weighed heavy with no illusion of a safety net.
By default I was an adult now. How terrifying. Let me
ignore this brutal fact with some good music and wait
this sweet wait until I hear Montana's knock at the door,
I think to myself on the way to the toilet.

My bathroom mirror bares the stroke of time like a
watch's face with no hands. A new crevice trivializes

53

age as a number. I look closer at the wrinkle, this time with trepidation. It is a cliff I could fall off of. Middle-aged is the peach that gets passed over for fresher fruits. "But what of her insides?" No one asks. No one cares. Kidneys go bad at the rate of falling breasts . . . broken hearts, too.

I interrupt my correspondence with reality to check the lottery. It is up to twenty million this week. At a dollar a ticket, a fantasy ride to the best plastic surgeon to remove the tides of flesh from around my throat is a bargain.

16

EIGHT O'CLOCK CAME and went. Montana neither called nor appeared. She must have a serious problem. She wouldn't just stand me up without calling. Pride is an artificial emotion, I convinced myself. I called with nothing to lose, except my smile. She answered nonchalantly. "My daughter borrowed the car. I lost your phone number. I had no way of getting to your place. " At this point, and at this point alone, I would never know her better. How lame! Irresponsible! Conflicted, passive-aggressive, manipulative, dependent . . . "Could you pick me up?" she asks.

"Sure. I'll be over in a few minutes," I respond. "How do I get there?" Under the guise of understanding I reason she is afraid. It is the only way I can see her again without being angry. I run to her suppressing my fear of a story that has no beginning.

I entered her life as I stepped through the front door. She welcomed me with the scent of fresh makeup and shampooed hair. Our eyes avoided each other. They might say too much too soon. I moved with her as she looked for the rest of her things. The rhythm was there. The dance had begun.

We took a route along the sea's raggedy edge. A whiff of the night air with a touch of salt carried us to a Mexican restaurant in the corner of a vacant mall. The shoppers had long gone home leaving a ghostly feel to the place. At last two planets seated, separated only by a bowl of guacamole. Her face took up the entire restaurant. I was an astronaut about to walk on the moon and plant my flag somewhere on the top of her head. "So, tell me who are you and would you have had dinner with me if you knew I was gay?" We laugh a hard laugh. Was it that funny? I wondered.

In the weeks that followed, our friendship deepened. Toasting early Sunday mornings with croissants and mimosas from inside a cove, leaving the stone walls only when dispossessed by the wash of high tide. A kiss archived in a cave hidden from the sun. We were wet. We were in love. We painted each other into our lives, onto our canvases . . . She sold a painting and we celebrated at the Ritz. I sold a painting and we celebrated again. "Two Remi Martins, heated please." Two glass bubbles on fire. I imagine that if you could swallow love it would taste like cognac. Two menopausal adolescents recalcitrant by nature, spontaneously throwing rolls of toilet paper at each other in the middle of supermarket aisles. She was the other side of me.

But at night we would go home to our own beds, leaving our hearts behind. Ever-so-tender fantasies emerged as I made love to my sheets. Oh, for the ruby-red bead between us. She was afraid to love another woman, but consumed by the desire. I was afraid the war inside her would turn against me. The love between two women is not a part-time affair. Casual does not apply. There are no back rooms to jerk each other off in. There are no stalls for anonymous sex. The primary sexual organ is the heart. When stimulated, however, it does not turn hard.

17

IT WAS COLUMBUS Day. Montana and I were shopping in Berger's Department store in Los Angeles. She was looking for a bra large enough to house two handfuls without framing them in an underwire. A good buy brings out the competition in women. I approached the lingerie table when a flock of silk birds flew by with size D cups. The sale was hot. I offered Montana a piece of chocolate, which she inhaled without taking her eyes off the runway. She had just spotted Victoria's secret with wings outstretched, iridescent and shiny, a rare find. She tried to grab it but was too slow for the greedy shopper also in need of support on the other side of the table. I retreated knowing full well the meaning of a good sale.

Later, we met at the cash register. Paid in full, we walked through two glass doors that opened magically. Suddenly, the magic was gone. An ugly little woman forced her way in between us, insisting that we were under arrest for shoplifting. "There's a mistake," I tried to convince her.

She refused to listen. Instead, she grabbed Montana. "You come with me," she dictated, pulling Montana's pocketbook out of her arms.

"Why are you doing this? What did we do?" I pleaded with the gnome to stop while Montana fought to hold on to her personals.

"The chocolates," muttered the gnome.

"The chocolates? Please, let her go," I shouted. "She didn't do it. It was me. I took them, two or three from an open box that was broken. It looked like it had been through the war. Please, it's my fault. Let her go. I'll pay for them," I begged.

In the midst of the chaos Montana hauled off and

socked the wretched creature in the face, drawing a crowd of vultures ready to forgo a good sale for cheap drama.

Then we were in deep shit. Montana refused to accompany the detective back into the store. Instead, she took off into the mall. The detective shouted to Montana: "I will have you hung for this!"

"But it's my fault!" I yelled at the venomous squirt. I screamed it, but it changed nothing. Sheryl Holmes, that was her name, escorted me back into the store while Montana hid in the dark corners of the mall waiting for me to be freed. Handcuffed, I was hauled off to a torture chamber on the top floor. While we waited for the police, Sheryl showed her prisoner off to the staff.

"I got one of them, all right," she said proudly. Meanwhile, I glanced at the mock newspaper headings plastered across her office walls: SHERYL, GREATEST STORE DETECTIVE IN THE WORLD. SHERYL, NUMBER ONE INVESTIGATOR AT YOUR SERVICE.

Finally, Officer Dillon arrived, his guns well hung but out of proportion to the size of his head. Looking young enough to be in high school, his youth lent a dry humor to the bizarre evening. Blushing, he charged me with an infraction saying, "Montana is the one we really want." She was on the "Ten Most Wanted List" for eating a piece of chocolate I stole.

But punching the store detective in the face was only the prelude to the evening. "We found your friend hiding in the mall. When we tried to take her in for questioning she bit my partner's ear and kicked his balls in. Yea, she's gonna pay for this," the cop insisted.

First she was a victim of my impulsive taste for chocolate, now she was a felon. The charges against her were petty larceny, resisting arrest, and assault and battery of an officer and a detective. I found her late that night behind bars. Encrusted in dry mud and tears, her anger had turned to sadness. I posted bail and took her home.

In bed for the first time, we spent what was left of the early morning together. I was inside out with guilt. I held her head to my heart and cradled her hurt with my breasts. I bathed her tears in chamomile tea and soaked her feet in a bath of roses. I placed lilacs on her tongue and filled her ears with the sound of velvet.

But to no avail. Montana blamed me from start to finish. If not for me, it never would have happened, she insisted. The next day she placed her "hello" on her answering machine and refused to speak to me.

How criminal there are no sentences for broken hearts but only stolen chocolates. How easily I confused the pain of rejection for the intensity of love. Abandonment, desperation, then rage consumed me. She found me guilty and exiled me from her court. I was no longer her love but a used-car saleswoman with each failed attempt at contact.

How did Montana turn my small infraction of the law into a felony? The question haunted me. When she was a kid she would fall asleep to the cries of her sister in the next room. She was terrified her turn would come . . . One still night a depraved cop—her stepbrother— hunched over her small body while she slept. Nestling his head in her neck, pulling at her arms . . . the cries in the room became hers. Her mother looked the other way because life was beautiful and everything was just fine.

Now enter Detective Sheryl, now enter Officer Dillon. Push and pull on her again. Stimulate memories buried in the muscles. Kick off the terror of authority, abuse authority with more abuse, shatter trust by refusing to listen, and then wonder why Montana doesn't trust the system.

18

ONE ATTEMPT TO contact Montana led to another as one day led to another. But I was running in place. There was no way back to her.

I knew exactly what I needed. I dreamed of a BLT with a pickle on the side and some cole slaw in a small white cup . . . an egg cream also, please. Simple. The round bar stool with the ripped leatherette seat, relieved of all pretense. The white cotton stuffing coming out from the cracked red vinyl, forgiving. "Wadda ya want?" The waitress asked. "I want to go home," I told her. She scurried off to the short-order cook, returning with an empty plate. There were no luncheonettes in Stolen Ridge . . .

I missed New York sorely, especially my friend Annie. With no tears to lubricate the loss I sailed a dry sea. The ebb and flow of what was, the convulsive rippling of my heart left me homesick. Montana proclaimed she was forever heterosexual and no longer ate chocolate of any kind.

I already had one foot out of Stolen when I received Annie's letter. It was a sunny morning like any other in Southern California. One more sip of coffee, a touch of early morning Bach and I was ready. Preserving her lick, I tore the side of the letter off rather than forcing the flap from the envelope. I was just easing into the note when the jolt catapulted me back to New York.

Cloe,
I went to Soho yesterday. Cloe, you won't believe this—the Gropel went bankrupt. They lost their gallery on Greene Street and are desperately selling off their inventory. Your paintings are on the street—right on the corner of

Spring and West Broadway. They are practically giving them away.

What are you going to do? Can I help? I miss you terribly. Will you come home?

Love Annie.

Going cross-country was the adventure, returning was the defeat. I retraced my steps back to Manhattan hoping to pick up the pieces of my life. The Gropel had gone bankrupt without contacting me. They were selling my paintings for a fraction of what our contract stated. I found an attorney who took a painting in lieu of payment and filed a lawsuit against the owner. But lawsuits take time . . .

The phone bills were cheaper now that I was back. Annie and I spoke almost daily. Finally, she told me she was divorcing Curt, her husband. Then she broke down, "The truth is he is divorcing me. Can you believe it?" she said. "The bastard is fucking a twenty-year-old. He met her rollerblading. Apparently, he crashed into her in Central Park. He used me up and threw me away after he tripped on her. I feel so old." I felt Annie's pain. I wanted to make it better for her but the most I could do was listen. She told me that was a lot.

In the interim I built my practice. We have two lives, I remind myself, I remind my clients . . . the one our mother gave us and the one we give ourselves.

Anastase Wright

WHETHER HE BELONGS to a different species that is yet to evolve or is really just another mortal is academic. The point is while hordes of women are searching for Mr. Right on the Internet, hoping to attract his attention with an ad at least as clever as their counterparts, he sits firmly on my couch at this hour, on this day, for an initial consultation. He tells me his name is Anastase Wright.

A visibly generous cranial capacity serves as a backdrop for a shapely face that gently pushes forward, setting off a chiseled nose that projects a refined sense of smell. All under the abundant shade of two massive brows, squared off by a chin conspicuously designed to give the appearance of Paul Newman's younger brother. About six-foot tall, a stunning intellect overshadows his physical presence. His age is difficult to discern. He tells me he is forty-six and that he grew up on the upper West Side, across the street from the Museum of Natural History.

The commitment of getting to know someone at their core breeds an alliance that takes time. Initially, I observe him with keenness generally reserved for an electron microscope. There is something familiar about this man. He appears puzzled when I ask if we have met before and flatly denies the possibility. However, at fifty minutes, once a week, for as long as it takes I am confident the connection will surface if there is one.

Professional reserve belies my curiosity while he tells me why he has come to see me. "I believe I have an immutable problem I am at a loss to change. Medically it's termed 'Sleep Apnea' or the implacable tendency to snore. It has destroyed my love life. I can't sleep with anyone in my house, much less in my bed.

Have you ever slept with a thunderstorm, Dr. Goldwin?
. . . Not through a thunderstorm, Dr. Goldwin, with one?
I have undergone radical surgery with one of the top surgeons in the city but I still snore and wheeze now, too. I guess I can only learn to accept my fate and endure a sentence of intolerable loneliness." His words come easily, too easily for such despair.

"I see. And you blame your snoring." Not buying into his rationalization but not wanting to knock it just yet, not before we've established a trust, I ask him if he can tell me a little more about himself.

"Actually, I saw your ad in the *Village Voice*," he says, clinging to a weathered tote bag snuggled at his side. "I thought it a brash attempt at solicitation, however, to the point."

I rethink my ad while Anastase gropes with getting closer to his real problem.

19

HOOKED ON HOOKERS?
For therapy call Dr. Goldwin
212 888-0000

AT THE TIME, I reasoned a more "professional" ad for sexual conflicts, which is one of my areas of specialization, sounds stiff, sterile, hard to relate to. It promotes the very anxiety therapists are trying to absolve. In this time of commercialization why shouldn't one put it as it is? One is not "Addicted to Prostitutes" when one is "Hooked on Hookers," is one?

After wrestling with which knee to cross, Anastase begins. "Well, it's difficult for me to concede but I'm 'Addicted to Prostitutes.' I immediately hold back the temptation to paraphrase his words. A long silence follows. Then he continues. "Aren't you going to ask what I get out of, shall we say, my wanton devotion?"

"Do you require permission?"

"I'm a sensualist of edible delights that become unwrapped for a fee slightly higher than the price of chocolates," he says. "Each moist filling a gustatory delight of woman flavors, luscious, ranging from mild to piquant. A nip, a pinch, a bite, a veritable . . . Have you ever been to a whore, Dr. Goldwin?"

The question coupled with a hard vacant stare unsettles me. "By virtue of my sex the opportunity has passed me by. Tell me, what are your feelings about seeing a female therapist?" I ask knowing his conflicts with women are profound.

"My mother was a female . . . there was very little we didn't share, but that's the hook isn't it? That's really what you want to know. It all goes back to mom, doesn't it?" He is attuned to the process as if he had been in therapy before.

"She would tuck me in like other mothers. I would feel safe and warm under a heavy woolen blanket. Then, in the middle of the night, when I was fast asleep, she would wake me up. 'Anastase,' she would whisper, not wanting to scare me, 'did I tell you what they did to little boys who didn't listen?' I would cringe at the sound of her voice. 'Do you know how far you can freeze a human being before they're frozen, Anastase?' She would ask me these questions while foraging through a bunch of tattered photos she hid under my bed. It might be two, three in the morning. 'Itzak's mother Becky wondered what the limits were. The Nazis used her son to experiment on. We were in the death camp together. Did I tell you, Anastase?'

"My mother couldn't forget the horrifying details of the concentration camp. She would recall savage stories to me the way a mother reads Hansel and Gretel to a child. Over and over again I was put to sleep by these fairy tales.

"'Becky was desperate to know what happened to her son. She was a good woman, Becky was. She wouldn't give up. One day—are you listening, Anastase?' she would say. 'Becky learned the details from an informant in the laboratory for the price of . . . well, I'll tell you about that some day when you're old enough.' I was already old, I thought to myself. I am six years old. "Here, Anastase, look!' She pulled a worn photo out of her pile of horrors. The image disintegrated through her fingers as she spoke. 'See, Anastase that was her son Itzak, before the experiment.' The faded tones of sepia took on the shade of brown blood as the boy's leg crumpled off the rest of his body. His eyes were the closest thing to flesh, his toes were mangled by a Nazi for not standing straight enough when he passed by. This photo was before the experiment, before the Nazis froze him. The boy was my age. He could have been me—a skeleton of me. It sucked the warmth out of my blanket. It chilled me dead cold. I slept over their graves, begging my mother to store the corpses somewhere else—but not under my bed. She refused. They were too precious for her to move. She saved thousands of gruesome photos after the war. She would cut them out of magazines, newspapers . . . anywhere she could find them. That was her childhood— her family album.

"Afterward, she would kiss me good night. 'It's all right, Anastase,' she would comfort me. 'It's all right. Go to sleep now son. Tomorrow is a new day.' It was never a new day. She was a survivor with a swollen memory she could not let me forget."

Wrapping a sweater around my shoulders, I feel his pain. "You are also a survivor of your mother's swollen memories." Anastase pulls back from the pain he suddenly feels through me.

"Can you tell me about your father?" I ask.

"I never knew my father," he answers abruptly. "He was, well, a one-night stand. My mother never hid that from me. I was her confidante first, her son last." Indignantly, he recounts his history as if it were someone else's. "After the war my mother did what she did to survive, Dr. Goldwin. She was alone, a gypsy girl who managed to get to New York City after the war but had nowhere to go once she arrived. She had no relatives, no friends, and then she had me." Anastase fidgets with the handle of his tote bag.

"What did your mother do to get by?" I ask.

"I grew up in a brothel, Dr. Goldwin. As I said, she was a survivor, a strumpet, a trollop, a whore to be more exact. My childhood is unique that way, don't you think, Dr. Goldwin? My 'aunts,' my 'baby-sitters,' my 'family' as my mother called her 'colleagues' were all 'ladies of the night.' And, I was the 'darling' of the house, that's what they would call me."

A conspicuous absence of emotion veils his torment. It is the same detachment that characterized his mother's stories.

"That's all there is to tell, Dr. Goldwin." No longer needing my prompt he continues. "As the 'darling' of the house I was frequently called upon, in secret, to service the Madam of the house, Regina. If I ever told, she warned, my mother would lose her job and the small room we lived in, in the back of the parlor. That meant we'd be homeless. At first, I was her student, a student of fellatio. Then a master . . . not in lying Dr. Goldwin, as in 'fallacious" [which he spells out] but as in sucking the dicks of johns that happen to have had a predilection for little boys. Do I have your attention Dr. Goldwin?" He asks knowing full well he has my attention. The coldness of his rage concerns me. After listening to his story I am struck by the glaring disparity of how accomplished he appears given his history.

Anastase anticipates my observation. "I guess you're wondering how it is that I am not entirely mad, aren't you?"

"That would be an accurate assumption," I think to myself. "Tell me, have you ever been in therapy before?" I ask, attempting to get more of a history.

Anastase looks me straight in the eyes. "No, Dr. Goldwin, I never have been in therapy." There is a flat, unflinching coldness to the quality of his response that gives way to a quick turn in the road.

"Did you know that dinosaurs are birds, Dr. Goldwin? They have three primary toes on both of their feet and an S-shaped neck. The theory is based on cladistic analysis, a system that organizes animals according to the unique characteristics they share. It's reconstructed phylogeny. Because of it, extinct species like dinosaurs aren't isolated from earth's history."

"You identify with the dinosaurs and the loneliness of extinction," I suggest, feeling a profound sadness, a sadness he won't let himself feel.

"You see, Dr. Goldwin," he continues, "while other kids went home to milk and cookies on plastic table-cloths served by mothers in rollers and floral-colored aprons, I hung out in the splendor of prehistoric life. The Museum of Natural History was my real home. I slept at the cat house on 77th Street but I lived in the Halls of Dinosaurs. I ate dinner alongside the largest carnivore to ever walk the earth, Tyrannosaurus Rex. I did my homework beside hadrosaurs like Anatottan, duckbill for short. And when I cried, I cried with Edmontosaurus, a dinosaur mummy who gave the impression he had skin. That always endeared me to him. It all makes sense though, doesn't it? I mean, if one is going to trace the descent of their ancestors, particularly their paternity, why not start at the beginning?"

Clever, I think to myself.

"I remember asking my friend Sammy—he was a guard in the museum, at the Theodore Roosevelt Rotunda—how old Ed was. 'Well,' he said confidently, 'Ed is sixty-five million, twenty years, four months, two weeks old.' Stunned, I asked, "How can you tell the date so accurately?" 'Well,' he said, 'Ed was sixty-five million years old when I started working here. That was twenty years, four months, two weeks ago.'"

Caught by surprise and the charm of his humor, we laugh. "Sammy almost always made me laugh . . ." He says. "Anyway, by the time I was a teenager I knew every dinosaur by their first name. After all, these guys were my relatives. I knew what they ate, how they ate, whom they ate. It got me a full scholarship to Columbia."

"And now? What do you do?" I ask.

"Well, what if I told you I am a professor at NYU, in the anthropology department. My research is in anthropophagy . . . cannibalism, that is."

There is a fraction of a smile in Anastase's eyes, a tenderness he keeps safely hidden. To my own surprise

I wish we could continue when, suddenly, the fifty-minute hour is up. Anastase rises abruptly with tote bag in hand, saving himself the rejection that comes with having to be reminded to leave. I take my pen in hand as he closes the door. I know this man but I don't know how.

20

"DR. GOLDWIN?" A stranger called from the intercom, his words muffled by the sounds of the street. "My name is Jack Demson. I need to talk to you. Please, let me up."

At first I thought he was a client responding to my ad in the *Voice*. "I don't see clients without an appointment," I said. But he sounded distressed and I had a few minutes. Once I retrieved him from downstairs I took the lead, asking him a few preliminary questions to expedite the process. "Mr. Demson, I have only a few minutes before my next appointment. Would you like to tell me what the nature of your sexual problem is?"

"Ugh, Dr. Goldwin I, I . . . "He stuttered for a moment before I cut him off.

"That's OK, Jack, let's schedule an appointment when I can give you the time your problem requires." I was shocked when he overcame the impact of our initial misunderstanding to reaffirm his virility.

"Dr. Goldwin," he said pulling out his shiny badge. "I'm Detective Demson from the major case unit at One Police Plaza. If you are so clairvoyant perhaps you can tell me where your friend Annie Marshall is. Her ex-husband told me you were one of her best friends."

"I'm confused. Has something happened? I don't understand . . ."

"We have reason to believe your friend is in serious trouble."

Feeling the gravity of her disappearance in the pit of my stomach, I apologize profusely. "Oh God, Detective. I hadn't heard from her in more than a week, almost two. I called a few times but she wasn't home. I just assumed she was busy. I should have known something was wrong. What is it, Detective? What's happened?"

"Can you tell me when you saw her last?" Demson continues questioning me. He knows he has the right of way.

"Of course," I said, pausing to remember our last meeting. "It was three weeks ago. Annie and I had met for a cappuccino at Dean and De Luca, the one in Soho." That's where we usually met, I thought to myself, remembering we were in between clients that day and had an hour to spare. It was a sweltering day. She was wearing a loose-fitting pair of slacks, linen I think, and an oversized man-tailored shirt, rolled up at the sleeves. She was self-conscious about her weight. Her baseball cap said "Go For it" and she did. "How can I possibly have dessert," she said, ordering a slice of chocolate mousse cake in the same breath. She laughed about her guilt . . . the way it hung from her thighs.

Ensconced in the "art heart" (that's what we'd call it joking around) we took a break from problems in living. How nice the break was, I remember telling Annie. We were sitting next to an art dealer at the time. "Can you believe it," he was telling his colleague, "Madonna sends her manager to buy a painting. She can't be bothered to come down to the gallery and see it for herself. Bowie came down himself just yesterday. He's real."

"We talked about the usual—art, love, psychodynamics . . . the Picasso exhibit at the MOMA. Menopause. The pros and cons of hormones. She said they were inflating her belly. I said they were inflating my breasts. She said she was going to revise her life. I said I was working on accepting mine. I mean she was in good spirits. In fact, she almost glowed. That was the last time I saw her."

"Did she give you any indication that someone was bothering her? Maybe a disturbed client? Was she planning a trip?"

"No, not at all. I mean it is August, that is when most shrinks take their vacations. But neither of us talked about leaving the city. Annie would have told me if she was going away. We told each other everything ..." Not to would be a deep violation of our bond, I thought to myself. "I wish I could be more useful, Detective," I said, recalling the secrets we had shared. Remembering how upset she was twenty years ago when she took her first apartment. After she signed the lease, the landlord reminded her that they didn't allow dogs. Annie never forgave herself for not reading the small print first. Not just because she was inexorably attached to Muffy. Truth was she had trained him to go down on her. When I asked how she did it she told me she used chopped meat. After that, there were no secrets between us.

"What else can you tell me, Dr. Goldwin?"

Keeping that one to myself, I continue, "Annie was going through a lot. Her husband wanted the divorce. It was messy once they started divvying things up like the co-op, the summerhouse in the Hamptons, the BMW. It's funny how the material things that give you the greatest pleasure become the source of greatest angst when a marriage has run its course. At least they didn't have to worry about custody rights. They never had kids. Actually, Annie was feeling liberated from an oppressive marriage once she got over the shock. She was looking forward to a fresh start."

"What can you tell me about her husband?"

"Curt? Curt's a workaholic, a lawyer, the kind you love to hate. He wanted to take everything from her even though she put him through school. She supported him until he became a senior partner in a prestigious law firm. He is a crackerjack attorney. But there's a sadistic edge to him . . . kind of passive-aggressive personality."

"What do you mean by that, Dr. Goldwin?"

"Well, he is strange. I mean, I remember once we went out to dinner at Raoul's on Prince Street. Curt laid these gruesome autopsy photos of dead naked women on the table, just before we were about to eat. He got a vicarious thrill out of the brutality of the photos and ruining our appetite."

"Obviously a thrill he couldn't contain," the detective notes.

"But I never thought of him as dangerous," wondering if that were true after I said it.

"But he could be, wouldn't you say, Dr. Goldwin?"

My fear is settling in my stomach. Feeling pressured by the interrogation, I admit it's possible.

"What do you know so far?" I ask, choking back my tears.

"Actually, her Curt called the bomb squad. Said he received a suspicious package, thought it was sweating. That's a telltale sign for a package bomb, you know. Especially, to someone in the field. Explosive devices are oiled just before they mail 'em to make sure they go off smoothly. Sometimes they leak. He says he didn't realize Annie was missing till we opened the package. Apparently they are already separated."

"I'm lost. A package? What package?"

"The package contained a letter and a pound of flesh—fat to be more exact, wrapped in a plastic bag. The bag broke. Most of the print on the return address is smudged, even the postmark. You can barely make the letter out but here, see if it means anything to you. The graphologist already verified the handwriting. It's Annie's." The detective hands me a urine-colored paper with a rancid smell, repulsive to touch.

> *Dear Curt,*
> *SMUDGE*
> .... *tortured*
> *me.......life.   SMUDGE   won't   let*
> *SMUDGE......................controlling my every*
> *move. My body SMUDGE . SMUDGE took*

everything from me SMUDGE. I cannot
live.......... SMUDGE.................................. to
death. SMUDGE.............drained dry..... I
want SMUDGE......what's left of me.
      SMUDGE yours,
      Annie

The floor inside me quakes. Clinging to the letter only makes my heart pound harder. Is this for real? Annie abducted? Not Annie. Not Annie. Held against her will, starved, tortured, mutilated, with no idea of what is going on? I am numb, trembling, the letter shakes in my hand. "I cannot make it out. What does this mean, Detective?"

"We're not sure. Could be an ex-con that's getting back at Curt through Annie, maybe for putting him away. Then again, it could be Curt, or one of Annie's clients, maybe some psychopath that had been stalking her for a while. We just don't know yet. But every con leaves their own signature at the crime scene. Deviant patterns of a criminal tend to remain consistent. We submit what we have so far to VICAP, the center for the analysis of Violent Crime, and they will send us a personality profile of the type of person that could be responsible for the offense, based on research of similar offenses. Meanwhile, the lab is checking out the package. If the abductor handled the fat first, before he mailed the package, grease will make the prints easier to pick up. The paper, the plastic wrap, the stamps, even the fat itself will be chemically analyzed. If there are prints we'll get them. Even the fat will be examined, whether it's animal or human, man or woman. That sort of thing. What doesn't jive is why the abductor let your friend send the letter but didn't protect it. Generally, these guys are obsessive about things like that. The Unabomber for instance, wrapped his package bombs meticulously over and over again with lots of stamps.

He wanted to be sure it was going to arrive intact. It's possible, of course, that who ever sent this package didn't want the letter to be legible."

"You mean a setup?"

"Perhaps. Well, we're examining all of her records. Her clients, her telephone calls. I hope you will make yourself available if we need any more information."

"Of course, Detective. Do you have any leads?"

"So far there are two similar cases in the city. We're beginning to suspect a pattern."

"Is there anything they have in common?" I ask, groping for a glass of water.

"We're not sure yet. No note, no package has turned up for the other two. But both of them are therapists from Manhattan and . . ."

The buzzer goes off and it's clear my next client has arrived. Short on time I escort Demson downstairs still reeling from the news and the slimy feel of the letter in my hands. "If there's anyway we can find her we will. Keep the faith. We'll be in touch."

As he passes my next client on his way out Demson gestures toward me. For a moment, I expect he is going to flirt with me as a final cliché to go with all the murder mysteries I've read. "Oh, by the way," he says, "the two other victims were both authors. Watch yourself."

"Sure," I respond. *Art Beyond Insight* is a book I just co-authored with Annie. It came out this month."

Caesar

THERE IS A gap between psychologist and detective. At the moment it is practically imperceptible. What was done and who did it is a backward journey for both professions. But now my understanding is tainted by suspicion. Symbols give way to clues and dynamics are motives.

Caesar, a new client, has no idea he is a suspect for murder. He is a tall man with a short man's personality. He tries to impregnate me with his thoughts from the start. "I am handsomer than most and smarter, too. That is my problem. You will agree (or I will leave therapy)," he insists.

When I resist his tongue stiffens. Gorged with opinions his pitch rises. "I am a truth seer. My perspicuity is razor sharp. You know that." My lips murmur "no, I think not." Instinctively, I resist his word sperms. I won't let him cum in my mouth or put words in there either. Now, the tiny dictator shouts to be heard. A siren sets off the alarm. "If you do not succumb to my reality I will get angrier till I burst and it will be your fault for not seeing things my way." He interprets the lack of agreement between us as disobedience. I am bad for not seeing things his way. He is convinced he has a monopoly on worldviews. He has no recollections of what formed the views but he is a loyal conscript to them, anyway.

"What you don't remember runs you. History is the driver," I tell him. You will have to dig into your past. The world does not support the grandeur of self-illusions." Then I think again. . . .

Therapy would have been frustrating for Napoleon also.

21

NOT AN HOUR goes by, not a moment that I am not thinking of Annie. I cannot accept that she is being held captive, cannibalized by a madman or woman. I remember my neighbor Greta and how she was found. To function under this stress, to balance the terror of her disappearance in between a broken heart and broken clients takes it toll. With all the fury pent up inside, my art takes a radical turn.

Finally, my day in court . . . The judge, a fair-haired man in an oversized robe rules in my favor. The Gropel Gallery violated our contract. They must return my paintings—all forty of them or compensate me according to our contract, immediately.

I am ecstatic. Eager to find a new gallery, I mail my slides in the typical tan envelopes, stamped and pre-addressed to minimize any undue expenses the galleries might incur in the rejection process. Finding a gallery does not come easy this time. The rejections mount. All my slides are returned, my name plastered on the envelope as sender and receiver as if I was playing a silly game with myself. Many slides come back without any acknowledgment, without a sign of ever having been looked at. I find this lack of courtesy particularly irksome. Already pained by Montana's rejection and Annie's disappearance, I write myself the letter they don't send:

Dear artist ha ha,
Thank you very little for submitting your slides.
We couldn't see how you dared to but we got
them anyway. We didn't bother to send you the
note you are now reading because we, as a
benevolent institution, didn't want to hurt you.

*We know how sensitive artists are. But it's
understood, isn't it? Please do not ask us to go
through this process again with you. Unless ,of
course, another gallery makes you famous.
Then please resubmit your slides immediately so
we can take a 50 percent cut of any work you do
sell in the future.*
We wish you the best of luck.
Love,
Leo Castelli and the rest of the gang

With nothing to lose, I decide to take charge of my
rejection. I walk down the same streets in Soho, West
Broadway, then Prince, over to Spring . . . Coolly, I will
insist on those letters of rejection from galleries who
didn't feel my effort was worth a note. Calmly, I enter
the sacred halls of Castelli's and approach Leo himself.
"Mr. Castelli," I address him with all the due respect of
a god, "would you be kind enough to provide me with a
rejection letter? A Xerox copy will do." How odd. He
refuses that which came so easily before and has me per-
sonally escorted out of the gallery.

But I am unrelenting in my mission. Paula Cooper
is my next stop. She requests a quick look at my slides
and then willingly complies . . . so does Nancy
Hoffman. "Gladly," she replies. "Of course," Charles
Cowles obliges me. "Indeed," Sperone Westwater con-
cedes. It's easy enough. By the end of the week I have
accumulated more than twenty letters of rejection, the
raw materials for my next project.

Now the fun begins. With scissors, some white-out
and a pen instead of a brush, I transpose each little hurt
into its opposite. Artists rejecting galleries. The return
address of the gallery is now in the salutation preceded
by the word Dear, of course. All rejections are signed
by the artists in the form of a photo, an assemblage of
painters including Rauchenberg, Johns, Picasso, Van

Gogh, Goldwin and others obscuring the gallery's original signature at the bottom of the page. The project is cathartic. I am renewed, jubilant.

The galleries, however, do not take their rejection well . . . But mine is confirmed.

Still, I am hanging between nowhere and nothing to lose. There are no words from Annie. Detective Demson says the lab has identified the fat as human. Annie's fingerprints are all over the fat, and the letter. There are no other clues. The postmark and the return address were completely obscured by the fat. They are still going through her records and will be investigating her clients.

Feeling as I do, I devise a plan that will change the meaning of "being hung." I burn my paintings (the word cremate is now difficult for me to use). With this radical approach, my resume boasts of my work at the major museums and galleries in town. However ashen, it is not a lie to say my work is at the MOMA. That it is buried in the sculpture garden is a fact I choose to omit. I do not bear false witness to say my work is at the Met. That it sits in the bottom of the toilet paper dispenser in the women's room is a trivial matter of location. Résumés never indicate where the work hangs, anyway. In the spirit of parsimony, with so many museums and galleries to include, my résumé is complete without such details.

However clever my attempt at conceptual art, I have exceeded the bounds of rejection. I am forever barred, undeniably, irrevocably finished. So say the gods who interpret my work as fraud. It is the end of a new beginning. Practicing therapy is my art now.

Ben

BEN WRESTLES WITH impotence. He is an irrational dis-ordered producer who despairs in the hopeless dream of ever winning an Oscar. Rachel, his wife, is omnipotent. Preferring Ann Klein to Calvin she makes more women pregnant in an hour than Ben could ever do in a year. This disparity contributes to Ben's emasculated self-image. While void of passion, their touchless, sexless marriage is a fecund union. Ben is a pornographer. Rachel is an embryologist. Although theirs is no mix-ing of the flesh, the meshing of their gears is reproduc-tive. God and Goddess, Ben and Rachel are primal Mom and Dad to a generation owing them their life, if not their genes.

Ben produces the hard-core porn that gives wannabe fathers their inspiration. Rachel brings each new video to the "Jerkatorium" with a secret pride. Ben is an inti-mate part of the process, which keeps her close to him. Gingerly, she handles each skin flick with as much care as she handles vials of sperm. "The 'ultimate Big Bang' is predicated on, if not propagated by his work," she acknowledges. Thus she bottles his reviews and freezes them with the utmost care, preserving "the sound of one hand clapping" for now and forever. It is the sound of a generation of fathers eternally grateful, and mothers too.

So much for the Oscar. "My plots, although sparse," he admits, "jump-start new life. The sperm spewing between the tender legs of my teenage nymphs," he says, "spawns an infinite number of chain reactions, culminating in one generation after another, an eternal population of ex-communicables conceived in sin and circumstance that I contrive . . . If not for my porn," he tells me, "they wouldn't be born."

Anastase Wright

ANASTASE IS PROMPT for his second session. The transition from outdoors is paralleled by an introspective shift in perspective. However awkward, Anastase offers a dream to cushion the landing.

"I had a dream last night that I have every so often. I thought it would be a good place to start. I rip a book apart. I don't even know why I'm doing it. I tear the pages up with my teeth until they bleed, stuffing the shreds into my mouth with both hands, like a hungry savage. I chew on the shreds, swallowing the words with the blood, spitting out what's left of the printless curds. Interesting, isn't it? I mean, there's a sexual sadism to it, don't you think, Doctor?" He might as well be saying, "Pass the salt, would you?"

"What else can you tell me about the dream?"

"I'm not sure." He answers unperturbed by his own violence.

"What kind of book was it?" I ask. Detective Demson's words ringing in my ears, ". . . both therapists (murdered) were authors."

"Don't know." His coy smile makes me think he's holding something back . . .

Ignoring the sardonic quality of his reply I continue. "Then, why a book, Anastase? What are your associations?"

"Well, not much comes up."

Evading my question, he goes onto another track. "But, how are dreams different from reality, anyway? I mean, what you'd give your life for one moment becomes a memory the next. Over time, both are subjugated to the depths of the unconscious. It's all the same, dreams, memories, fantasies. Ultimately, reality becomes unreality. The joke's on us. It's the humor of a higher consciousness, of course. In fact, we may be the characters in a dream of a higher order, playing out a reality that was never ours to begin with. Floating around in his or her id, like wontons in a bowl of soup. Wanton wontons at that." Although weak boundaries between reality and fantasy characterize a psychotic personality, Anastase's reality testing is intact.

"When I think of growing up in that cat house it was like living in a dark secret. Literally. The curtains were always closed. No friends. The constant fear of kids finding out my mother was a prostitute. And my side job—Regina's sexual accessory . . . My childhood was a nightmare, a bad dream that never happened. Actually, it wasn't that bad—just a bit different. It was a rather good childhood."

The glaring contradiction of his words marks a faulty self-monitoring system.

"Regina, the madam, was an avid reader. She had hundreds of books by everyone from Dosteyevsky to Phillip Roth. Most of them hardcovers. When the Johns were gone she'd take the jackets off the books and put them back on by morning, before she opened the house. Sometimes, she made me help her with that too, putting them back on, I mean. Obsessive-compulsive disorder, isn't that what you call it, Dr. Goldwin?" He asks with a certain audacity, to flaunt his knowledge. The gap between knowledge and understanding is the gulf he is swimming in. His detached predatory stare makes me uncomfortable. Intense and empty at the same time. It was as if he knew me, as if we knew each other. But the transmutation of his rage onto books begins to make sense.

"Tell me, was one of those books in your dream?" I ask.

Gently stroking the handle of his tote bag, Anastase shows neither pain nor relief. Speaking through his face as if it were a mask, he answers. "Of course, it's so clear. Isn't it Dr. Goldwin? I think it was rather considerate of me to protect Regina and my mother from my rage and displace it onto a book instead. Don't you? I mean since books have no feelings, anyway."

"Anastase, how are you feeling right now?" I ask, wondering if he can break through his numbness.

"Where's the beef, Doc?" Anastase skillfully evades my question once again. "You know, psychotherapy leaves me with the same empty stomach I had as a kid. How starved I was for a whole mother. I mean, two full breasts and what's left over in a cup of milk. Thank you! That's all I ever needed. Maybe that's why I prefer prostitutes to therapists. The process is so much more palpable. Compare the rotund sensation, the global warming of a bosom to a voluptuous insight . . . You see what I mean, Doctor. Therapy doesn't soothe the void, it only magnifies it. There is no contest. Although both professions are quite similar, you know."

"How so?" I ask, intrigued by the idea of being likened to a slut.

"Actually, mingling of the flesh is only slightly more costly than the baring of one's soul. Sex or intimacy. You can purchase either by the hour. You see, my lady of the day, or are you my lady of the night? It is almost 6:00 p.m., isn't it?"

"However charming your verbal prowess, it's no disguise for your anger, Anastase."

Avoiding an emotional response, Anastase attempts to assert himself intellectually, as if in competition with me. "Are you familiar with Melanie Klein, Doctor? I mean with her theories on envy and greed? I guess, she would say I don't love breasts at all. In fact, she'd say I hate them. No . . . She would say my envy and my greed go beyond hate, to a desire to destroy. Not just because the first two breasts I knew were so bewildered, so withholding, but simply because they weren't mine to feed myself with. They were outside my control.

Frustrating isn't it? Not to be able to feed yourself, I mean with your own breasts." His humor fails to cloak the extent of his hunger. It is hard to believe he has never been in therapy before. He demonstrates an astuteness that is otherwise perplexing.

In fact, Melanie Klein goes even further, I think to myself. She would say he devalues the therapeutic process, envious of good interpretations because he didn't make them himself, desiring to devour the therapist out of the same greed and envy he had towards his mother. Wanting to consume the breast, to become the breast, to emerge self-sufficient and avoid the painful frustration of dependency on an inadequate source of nurturance outside of himself. To avoid the original maternal failure.

A premature interpretation can be harmful, experienced as an assault, especially when there has not been enough time for a trust to grow. It is only our second session. I choose to let the pieces fall for a while longer, reserving my thoughts for later. Yet, it is clear a traumatized mother thwarted his dependency needs. It seems she was suffering from post-traumatic shock syndrome, reliving the horrific events of the Holocaust through him, reversing their roles, using him to quell her desperate need for security, making her son her mother, leaving him with the profound sense of helplessness, the helplessness she felt.

Anastase pauses and takes a breath, before he switches the subject again. "Do you know who my favorite dinosaur is?" For a moment, he regresses to the youngster that took refuge in the museum. Pulling on the strap of his tote bag with a nervous back and forth motion he goes on, "Coelophysis is my all-time favorite. She was a mean mother, though. Rumor has it she ate her kids. Their bones were found in her stomach."

"What is there about Coelophysis that makes her your favorite?"

"An abundance of herbivores, plant-eating dinosaurs, have been found, but Coelophysis, Coelophysis is a rare find. She wasn't just a carnivore, she was a cannibal. They fascinate me, you know. Perhaps, it's because I feel my mother devoured me. When she couldn't sleep, I couldn't sleep. When she was frightened, she frightened me. She sucked me in, she filled her void with me like I was stuffing. She was terrified by her own aloneness. And now I am."

The peculiar access I have to this flesh-eating specialist haunts me. Will I be his next victim? Or can he help me find Annie? Dangerousness is a murky question. There is no science, no rules to ascertain it with certainty. To date, a psychologist's gut is inadmissible evidence in a court of law, even if it's a trained gut with a Ph.D. Annie has been missing for weeks and the police investigation has made no headway. I consider asking him just a few questions, maybe, a profile of Annie's abductor based on his knowledge. But asking him to help would only re-enact the early drama of a desperate mother leaning on him. Or expedite my own peril. It would be a serious hindrance to the therapy either way, I think to myself when he rises from the couch. The hour is up.

"Dr. Goldwin, I want to thank you. It is, as you can imagine, so difficult for me to open up this way. But I think for the first time I am making progress." Anastase forces his words through a clay face. To be moved by the pretense is to fall into a gap between words and emotions. It is a dark pit.

"By the way, Dr. Goldwin, I seem to have forgotten my checkbook. Can I pay you next time we meet? I am so terribly sorry."

The business of payment is always ripe for interpretation. The fee was discussed in advance. Forgetting his check is passive-aggressive. Perhaps, it is a manipulation. But if he is Annie's abductor I do not want to threaten him in any way.   Foregoing the symbolism, I emphasize his return. "Yes, that is all right, Anastase. I will see you next week."

Upon his leaving, I call New York University to verify Anastase's position in the Anthropology Department. In fact, Dr. Wright, I am told, is a tenured professor, chairman of the department. I am relieved, somewhat.

SOME OF THE most important lessons we learn are on the toilet. I remember daily lessons on the art of letting go. With several books stacked between her legs, sprawled out on the hard cold tiles of the bathroom floor my mother would read "Rapunzel, Rapunzel, let down your hair." Along with the drama of each fairy tale and the sound of running water, I would attempt to gain control of my sphincter muscles. "Don't squeeze so hard," she would tell me, " just relax . . . now let it go. Gently now." The triumph over my own biology in concert with a happy ending was reinforcing. But letting go is still a problem for me.

Annie is still missing. Confidante friend sister of mine, there is no trace of her. I learn from Detective Demson that Curt has been maintaining a life insurance policy in her name for $1,000,000 in spite of their break, in spite of their mutual distaste for each other. Shattered by the implication, I want to run to a warm heart. I have never felt so confused and alone. Without Annie I feel friendless.

After one day too long, I bite off all my nails and call Montana. I still love her hard and deep. Our closeness left a path inside me that would always be there no matter how much time goes by, no matter how overgrown the path with weeds. Before I can stop myself, thin strands of tender heart flow through pinholes in a phone. She will come to live with me from the other side of love, she says. I don't believe her, but I go to the airport to pick her up anyway. Alarms go off inside my head about the relationship. I turn them into bells.

Purposely, I am two hours early. I want to savor the thrill of the wait. Our relationship will never be better than that wait. Her flight is delayed for two hours. The size of my body is too small to house the fluttering of a thousand nightingales. I am about to take flight— meet her halfway in the sky. The anticipation is boundless. I imagine a hundred ways to greet her. Settling on a whisper-soft "hello" I sit back and follow my thoughts.

John

JOHN IS AN Hasidic Jew who makes love to a bald wife through a hole in a white sheet. I am immediately concerned for his sanity, but he assures me that he is well and that I am simply not versed in the tenets of Judaism. He can only make love to his wife seven days after she has menstruated providing she has had a bath, that is, a Jewish bath called a "mikvah." A mikvah is ordinary water that has been made kosher by a prayer. An ordinary man who has been made special by the prayers of other ordinary men conducts the holy service. If no one makes this prayer the woman is dirty no matter how much soap she uses, no matter how many douches she takes, it is a sin to touch her. A sin John would never commit. John gets up every morning and he thanks God he has not been born a woman. He teaches his sons to do the same, not to do so would be another a sin.

John's other name is Mustache Joe, or Moshe for short. That's how the "girls" know him. Moshe fondles the breasts of ladies of the night and penetrates all but their hearts. He does this religiously, too. Moshe is a pious man. He tells me it is not against the religion to have illicit sex with a prostitute, as long as she is not a Jewish one. That is, it's OK as long as he is not defiling one of his own. It's in the Torah he says, and refers me to the specific passage. He does not ask if they are clean. He does not ask if they are HIV-positive. To do so would be rude. The deadly contradictions of such reasoning elude me. In this case, by this definition, "cleanliness is next to godliness."

23

MONTANA ARRIVES IN cowboy boots and a horse-skin jacket. Misplaced high-mountain princess, she won't give me her eyes, but I can wait. She is, after all, here with me at last. We will spend the rest of our lives together, she vows over her ambivalence, in spite of her homophobia. She is not gay, she states calmly, but she loves me like no other. We will fight the cellulite with early morning runs around Washington Square Park and paint our hearts out together. If I get old first, she will serve me tea and preserve my vagina in salty green olives—the ones with the red spots on them. If she gets old first, I will brush her hair before she sleeps and continue to cover her gray with fire red. I am replete with this understanding.

Scavenger of scavengers, Montana finds an old warehouse around the corner that has gone out of business and has vacated the building. Metal skeletons of a once-thriving factory haunt an endless space. Steel chairs with no cushions sit empty in front of hundreds of old Singer sewing machines that were used by the overused. Shelves upon shelves line the walls with abandoned memories of so many days, empty, wasteful of the years. Bales of leather skins and workers' hides grew old here. Their blood and sweat leave the air heavy. Their toil pastes the walls with grease. Montana insists we fill the loft with these sad relics. She can use them to make my house her home. I cannot deny her this, although I wish to. I never change the furniture. The fear of losing her is a weight I am constantly trying to balance with the weight of Annie's disappearance. Change is unsettling though, especially when the change is loss. Constancy is the stuff of my profession. Constancy is my product, not Singer sewing machines.

Goldie Locks

GOLDIE COMES TO see me in a full-length mink coat and a Chanel shopping bag that hangs ever-so-casually over her arm. From the top of the bag I can see the headlines of the *Enquirer.* Her silver-blonde locks show no roots. With her lipstick worn off from oh-so-many kisses, the red outlining of her upper lip is exposed. The line violates the natural curve of her lip like a lie everyone can see. She greets me for the first time. She is baffled by the stares she was getting downstairs from the corner crowd while she was waiting for the elevator. "The Chicks with Dicks (transsexual working girls) couldn't seem to figure out whether I was one of them or not," she mentions in passing. "On this corner of half-truths," I explain, "it's the odd man out." She gets the picture and we begin with the business of unfolding the years.

At first, she boasts of an ideal childhood as many do. It's not an uncommon tale. Frequently, it's the hallmark of someone who has never been in therapy before. How many of us have really survived our childhood unscathed? The lottery is more likely. What is her story? I wonder. She tells me another story, the one she tells herself, while I wait for the one closer to the truth. Goldie sleeps in the beds of strangers, but for more money than I can count. Five-hundred-an-hour johns are sometimes happy with just a kiss and a quick hand job, she tells me. Am I in the wrong business? I think to myself. Seems far more profitable to give head than to analyze them. But Goldie, with a B.A. in business from Columbia, just bought "the clientele" from an eighty-year-old madam, the oldest madam in the city. "The other girls will do the dirty work now," she tells me.

Goldie's mother is a science fiction writer. Her list of publications include the secret lives of plants on

Mars. Her father is a pediatrician with no lollies in his office. They still live in a big house in a small town. But what does that have to do with happiness? Goldie was a mistake, a sexual indiscretion her mother made when she was sixteen years old. Goldie's mother whipped her because of it. She whipped her hard and fast with the buckles on leather belts. She could not forgive her for being born.

It is clear. The cupboard was bare for Goldie. There was no comfort in being an unwanted guest in her own family. Nothing was right, nothing could be; not the floors she cleaned, not the beds she made, not the dinners she cooked. Her mother blamed her for everything, leaving her with nothing. It was all her fault. It was her fault that her father played with dolls; even that he played with Goldie, late at night, while her mother slept. "But he tried to make it better with lots of money and lots of candy," she explains, still trying to preserve his goodness. She blames herself rather than her father, for the sake of a father to love.

After years of abuse, Goldie tried to murder her childhood as her mother had. She jumped out of a window from the house but landed on her feet. When that didn't work she settled for liquid love. The kind that comes from a vial and a needle. That worked fine, warm and dreamy. That is, so long as the works were clean. Each bed she tried seemed right then. Each plate was hers. But now she fears for her life. AIDS makes it so. She is at twice the risk. Dirty needles and johns who've come unwrapped. Two negatives make a positive she fears.

Goldie is the invention of Lou Ann, her real name. Her silicone breasts come with the play toy she has become. They shield her heart from the loveless touch of strangers. What a doll. What a smile. I used to think the best barometer of self-esteem was the condition of your panties but in this case I could be wrong. Belied only by her upper lip, she is lost in an abyss of self-hate. I point out a direction. "See if you can catch the lies you tell yourself, you tell the world. Grab them. Bring them to the surface. Expose them bare. Wrestle the bastards to the ground. An old story has been running you. You're still daddy's little girl. You're still doing it for the candy. Good girl, bad girl. Untwist the paradox. Dare to like yourself enough to rage against your mother, against your father. Get real Goldie, and fix your lipstick."

24

I REFUSE TO believe I will never hear Annie's voice
again. Maybe I am in denial. Demson has been investigating Annie's clients. Other than the possibility of a
setup by her husband Curt, Charles Leroy, one of her
clients, is the only suspect they have come up with.
Brutally abused by his father, Charles' characteristics fit
the profile of a serial killer. Warped needs to control and
to get even are apparent from Annie's notes. He is a
first-born and a loner. He has a history of bed-wetting
and mutilating puppies as a teenager. Serial killers tend
to have a history of mutilating animals, Demson tells
me. If a kid doesn't get over it by the time they're
twenty, chances are they go on to humans. Charles is
also impotent according to Annie's notes. Perhaps, he
uses his knife instead of his penis. The client, however,
fiercely denies the allegations. And there is no evidence
to hold him.

I must get away from all this. Montana has never
been on a New York bus before. So we take a luxury
tour up Broadway. I scope out details of strangers that
remind me of Annie.

There's Annie's nose on someone else's face . . .
Look, that person has Annie's walk! When I find her
gestures on someone else, it gives me hope that she is
still alive.

The ride uptown feels like a safari in an open park.
I caution Montana. People push to get on the bus and
push again to get a seat. Then, even if they are sitting
on top of you they pretend you're not there. Everyone
understands it's just the way it is. Don't take it person-
ally.   Frequently, passengers are out of their minds,
some because they can't find a seat. I explain it's OK to
ignore them but not to laugh. If they see they have your

attention they will want your seat and then your love. A verbal exchange is optional. The risk is yours. The problem is that if they start talking they may never stop, which makes it hard to get off the bus without cutting them off. New Yorkers don't like to be rude, contrary to popular opinion. That is why they don't talk to strangers. I explain all this to Montana before we get on the bus.

Montana is still processing my instructions on how to ride a bus when a woman with bleached-blonde hair set in toilet paper rolls takes her seat next to us. A black leather miniskirt just covers her pubic hairs. She's about seventy years old. She tells us of her love affairs without our asking. She does not pause for a breath. Montana is fully prepared though, thanks to my comprehensive introduction. We are up to Ronald Reagan as the bus approaches 60th Street. "He was great in bed," she whispers, "but he insists on using a dildo. Sometimes, he went into the bathroom with it on and forgot it wasn't his. Then, he really got confused. Truth is," she tells us, "he's got alcoholic dementia, not Alzheimer's, but don't tell anyone else I told you. It's a secret," she whispers loud enough for the whole bus to hear.

"Our stop! 72nd Street," I say, cutting her off. We leave the lady talking to herself as we get off the bus without ever knowing who her rollers were for. Zabar's is just down the street.

Zabar's is a visual feast, a jungle of gourmet delights. A fish's one-eyed stare monitors your choices from a frozen bed of diamonds . No chocolates this time, of course. Foreign labels are eatable mysteries canned and processed. Long after the love is gone, the memories of who you tried them with for the first time is forever preserved.

After seven days and seven nights the hunger between us reaches its peak. Montana gets close up from behind her eyes and takes the leap. She warms my hand with her hand, from her heart, to my cheek. I set my lips on her lips for just a minute before they have a life of their own. The tenderness, oh for the tenderness. Our breasts accommodate our embraces, nipples erect with sensation, we press hard against each other. Slowly, ever so slowly, our tongues come to the door and exchange mouths. Saliva bathes the words in a mixed solution. "Kiss me, fuck me, I love you. I love you so much." Who says what from which heart? A feast of chaotic juices mingling. Our bodies make a rope tightly wound. Tender words bite at the freedom to be said. Finally, they fly. Caged birds set free. We unsheathe our bodies the way others take their clothes off. Arms and legs the same. I run my tongue along her seam until I find her blood berry red. I unzip her opening and suck her out till she finishes playing the last note of our love song. Till the last sigh, for the last moan I breathe. She is the other side of me. It's a crescent ship we sail, one smile between us. Destination: deep heart where same meets same and one on one is one.

I want to believe we are about to spend the rest of our lives together. I set up an adjunct to my practice and call it Creative Analysis. We will work together. I will conduct a thorough psychological work-up on each client that will reveal the sensory modality they favor for creative expression. For some it will be music, for others painting, writing, or doing handstands. Montana will assist me. Each client will be video taped with the utmost care as they work. In effect, the creative process itself will be used as an *in vivo* example for how each individual functions and processes personal problems. Afterwards, the three of us will view the video together, exploring it for insights.

With our first advertisement in the *Village Voice* we are in business. After a week of no responses our one and only client arrives at 6:00 p.m. sharp. He is wider than he is tall, prematurely bald, and the thumb in his mouth takes the form of a cigar. He is a major power-broker on Wall Street. An in-depth assessment reveals our very first client is an exhibitionist with an obsessive-compulsive personality disorder and sadomasochistic tendencies. He is riddled with guilt and feels out of control. His wife knows nothing of his unrelenting desire to take his pants off. "I can't control the urge. It controls me," he tells us. "I get off on the shock value. Is it possible, I mean would you be offended if I did it here with you?" Professionally, ever so professionally, we talk about his need to undress as a metaphor to be accepted by others and repel them at the same time—two forces diametrically opposed. I suggest we explore his compulsion through painting.

Deprived of the opportunity to expose his member under the tutelage of a dominatrix (obviously a misunderstanding) he does not return for his second appointment. No others call. We are out of business before we start.

Still, the love between Montana and me grows. Together, we paint to the beat of our hearts. We paint to the honking horns on 14th Street, to the early morning sounds of garbage trucks, to the solos of Pavarotti. It's all music. There are no bad notes. The morning coffee is sweet. When the phone rings it is a beat like any other . . . except this time it is her boyfriend. He wants her back. The painting stops. Our seamless union is ruptured. How many ways can you tell someone you love them? How many ways can you ask someone to stay? I try them all.

While Montana is getting her things together I slip into the bathroom to prepare a final piece of satire to keep myself from sinking to the bottom of my heart. She is packing when I re-appear. I stand before her unabashedly naked with one addition to my anatomy. I hope it will make the difference. A toilet plunger, the kind with the long wooden stick, protrudes rudely from a rubber nozzle cupped to my pubic bone, sucking on my pubic hairs with all its might. It is not funny enough to make her want to stay. It's not sad enough either. It is no use. She leaves her tears in a Perrier bottle in the fridge that I mistake for spring water. I gulp it down and choke on the salt that sticks to my throat. It leaves me with an unquenchable thirst.

I look around my loft, as if for the first time. Singer sewing machines, industrial tables, ugly metal shelves, bails of old hides . . . I am a lone immigrant seamstress in a vacated factory that's gone bust. I no longer speak English. I am lost in my own country. How did I let that happen? It wasn't just a lover I lost. It was the child, woman, friend that promised to love me till I die.

It's clear. She preferred a cock to my heart. Disemboweled, I take a fetal position in my bed to grieve. There is nowhere to go but back. Did I think, without thinking, that her heterosexuality would go away? Did I think it would make me less gay? I relive every last minute of our love till it bores even me. When I leave my bed it's almost one week later. Now I put my ear to broken hearts, a stethoscope would only get in the way. My clients speak from where I sit.

Dr. Star

MY MOTHER WATCHES my struggle from above. Her head moves back and forth on the horizontal as she witnesses my all-too-many failed attempts at love with the wrong sex. From an elevated state, she says she is sorry for any inconveniences her flawed parenting has caused me. Her guilt takes the form of a gift called Dr. Star. She sends him to me by way of my business cards in Mel's Boutique. Dr. Star is the perfect compromise. He has been designed in an ethereal lab for discontent mothers whose children have gone awry.

Dr. Star, King of Queens, was married to a dinge queen. "A dinge queen," he explains, "is a black drag queen. She had all the glitz and glamour that I adored, but no longer," he says. "We were together for fifteen years. She saved my life with her loyalty. If not for her monogamy, I would have died from AIDS. I met her when I thought I was gay. She was more beautiful that any woman I had ever known. She was foolproof. Her beauty was uncontested. A man will always make love to a woman even if the woman happens to be a man. And I was a man like any other with a woman like no other. But now I live inside a civil war. I'm not a homosexual. I never really was. I can't deny it. I am a woman who lusts for other women."

Dr. Star is a man. Dr. Star is a woman. Dr. Star is also a doctor, a Jewish mother's dream. He is an endocrinologist in the business of prescribing femininity itself, if you are willing to swallow the pill of it. "Estrogen, in combination with electrolysis, transforms hairy chests into buxom bosoms," he tells me. The rigid social convention of one sex or the other has made him rich. No one wants to be caught in between. It's either male or female. The waiting lists are long for those wanting to make a switch.

His swimming pool, in Beverly Hills, is larger than my loft, he tells me. It's trimmed in Greek columns and palm trees. Dr. Star says he is a lesbian. He isn't into cross-dressing. He doesn't swish his words. He doesn't posture.

Dr. Star is unusual, but when he asks me out he is well off the bell curve. However contrived, I am riveted to the possibilities this person represents; comforted by the sardonic twist heaven allows. It is obvious that Dr. Star is my mother's way of trying to make things right by me.

I give him my full consideration as one lesbian to another. My mother's celestial design is too perfect for me to ignore. He is tailored to my every need.

On the face of it, Dr. Star is a genetic male attracted to genetic females. Behind his nose, however, Dr. Star's reality is of a different sort. He has the heart and soul of a woman with a body that gets in the way. Dr. Star is the perfect ending to my story, as if born of *deus ex machina*. What if I run off with him into the sunset? I fly with him to Beverly Hills. I swim in our pool. I shop on Rodeo Drive for both of us. I even test fate and bear our children. But it's me who cleans the diapers and me who cooks our dinners. I change the sheets and then I think twice. Are we interchangeable? Language fails experience. Dr. Star slices rock-bottom assumptions. You don't have to be a woman to be a lesbian. You don't even have to be gay. However humbled by the invitation, I decline warmly . . . still fearing the dishes would be mine to do.

25

USUALLY BY 11:00 p.m. I am in bed. It was 10:00 p.m. on a Saturday night when I was already under the covers and happy to be there.

It was about that time when Paul called on his cellular phone. "Cloe, I'm in a cab on the way to the Algonquin Hotel. My date just pooped out on me at the last minute, I have tickets to see a great cabaret singer. Meet me there in fifteen minutes? You've got to get out, anyway. Come on, it'll be good for you."

Getting out did not seem half as hard as getting up. Half-asleep, already in a warm bed, and second choice at that, Paul's invitation was less than appealing. Paul could tell that I was in no mood to part with my covers but he would not take no for an answer. "Come on, Cloe. You can't isolate yourself like this. It won't bring Annie back and it only makes your love life worse. You'll love this singer. I'll meet you in the lobby. Hurry up," he insisted, giving me no choice.

I had met Paul years ago on a gambling casino that floated nowhere long enough to leave you with nothing to lose. This time I didn't expect a hundred dollars to last for more than five minutes. I was hostage to a twenty-five-dollar craps table with no cheaper tables around. Reluctantly, I squeezed in between a smoking cigarette stand who was building skyscrapers on the DON'T COME line and a handsome man with dark eyes that tunneled backwards. SEVEN COME ELEVEN. I was the head of a smoky green field tossing a hailstorm of fate cubes. SNAKE EYES. A ten-dollar Yo followed just as my chip hit the table. I won and won again. Now linked to the deep-eyed stranger betting on my throws, rooting on my side, I found myself in his arms with each win. Later, he would tell me how he prayed for those hugs with a screaming fate master out of control.

The casino faded into his bedroom with the dawn. Imperceptibly, the sampling of what was already a physical relationship followed. Seven Come Eleven the odds were on his side. He would pass the Come Line but what about me? I was willing to overlook his hairy chest for the experiment. The stage was set. All except for one minor detail . . . a rain hat for "Johnny."

It is amazing how fast a man can put his pants on. Almost as fast as he can take them off when it comes to sex. With no time for shoes Paul ran breathlessly out of the condo and down the road to a 7-11 store. There was no stopping him . . . except for the sign and the clerk that prohibited him from entering the store barefoot. "Fuck this," he repeated mercilessly as he stood outside the glass doors panting, waiting for the right someone to do him a favor. But at this hour there was only one possibility—a gray lady hunched over to see the sidewalk first, as if her back was broken by the weight of her age. The old woman emerged with a bottle of Mylanta for a bad case of indigestion. Seven come eleven, Paul hit on a winner. "Of course, son," she said with an all knowing twinkle in her eye. "Glad to see you're not gambling with your life." The unlikely accomplice was grateful for the adventure.

Paul agreed he would wait outside. Peering through glass windows he watched confusion twist the clerk's face. "Ribbed or plain?" It was hard to read the young boy's lips but Paul was almost sure that was his question. The wrinkled widow chose ribbed, of course and exited triumphant. Thanking her profusely Paul bent down, twisting his head just below her face to see her eyes. She smiled graciously and he was out of there.

Sweating semen Paul ran back down the road with the latex contraband. Home at last, tossing his clothes off, pulling his pants down, desperate for this very moment the rubber disappeared. Under the clothes? In his pockets? On the floor? Where the hell was it . . . ? Finally, he found it on the table where he put it.

Still sweating and out of breath from the run Paul jumped into bed. Anxiously, he stretched the recalcitrant rubber over a wilting pole—a disappointing scene to watch. Suddenly, the odds had changed. He had found the condom but lost his erection. "I prefer women anyway," I said, trying to make him feel better. After all it was his preference, too. But there was no consoling Paul. Anyway, that is how we became friends.

The Algonquin Hotel, a mausoleum on 44th Street off Fifth Avenue, preserves the spirit of dead intellectuals. One enters the lobby of the hotel like entering a time warp. A sense of being out of place is usurped only by the experience of being out of time. One is immediately struck with an eerie sense of intruding on a closed circle of friends. The spirit of a coterie of writers like Dorothy Parker and David Benchley are preserved in slightly worn colonial chairs that are carefully timed to the smell of musty tapestries. It's clear from the awkwardness of the chairs that the patina of the 1940s is maintained not so much because it was a beautiful time as because it will never be again. To the left of the registration desk I notice a blow-up of the cabaret singer, Anita Amorichi. Suddenly, I am awake by just the sight of her.

Paul had already secured our table and was waiting for me in the Oak Room. We didn't see each other often but when we did it was always pleasant. He was a man whose three-piece suits, usually Armani's, wore him well. "Like the table?" He asked. "I greased the maître d's palm for it."

"Guess we couldn't be much closer," I said. Our table was practically on what little bit of stage there was. I much prefer being in the audience to stage fright but I kept this thought to myself. It is after all, hard to dine with abandon when chewing the blood-red steak on your fork competes with the vocalist singing her heart out.

I was grateful. Anita entered the room after dessert. She was a bride so eager to start the ceremony she forgot about the groom. Her long satin gown swept the floor, reflecting the glow of the audience. It was a mutual love affair. Entranced, we were her groom, as she took her place in front of the Steinway piano. The lights dimmed, deferring to Anita's incandescence.

First one song, then another, gesturing towards me as she sang, she sang to me alone. Come rain, come fire, come the maître d', Anita was making love to me on stage with a total and absolute disregard for anyone who knew it. "Can't Dance, Don't Ask Me," "What is This Thing Called Love," "You'd Be So Nice to Come Home To," the audience faded out, as she offered the center of her eyes to me on a velvet tray . . . a hummingbird's tongue. Beyond her pupils, a long dark hallway led directly to her heart, descending into a moist tender place that had no end.

I was mesmerized by the gift she made of her melancholy. Each note a tear, each smile a chord of sadness that made you want to run with her to the end of the world, do anything for her, just to make her happy.

Taking a moment to reaffirm reality, Paul turned and asked, "Why isn't she singing to me that way?" The answer filled me like a helium balloon. "It's me she wants, Paul. Do you believe it?" At the end of the set she took her place on the side of the lobby to sign autographs and exchange niceties with her admirers. Like a dancer I waited in a corner for the right beat. At last, we locked eyes from opposite ends of the room. The beam of light that joined our eyes parted the crowd as I made my way to her. Her arms opened to a wide circle with a break just large enough for me to complete.

"You sang like you were singing to me, Anita," I

said suspended in disbelief and the smell of her perfume.

"I was, I was." She said. "It's your gaze. I mean you can sing to some people and they look away or their faces just bore you. But your face, I just got lost in it."

Suddenly, I had no past. No hurts. No scars. Only her smile. "Please, would you take my card."

"Oh, you're a psychologist. I can use one of those."

A side of my heart sank. Maybe she just needed someone to sing to. Singers do that. "It's not that I think you need a psychologist. Maybe I just need a singer." We laughed hard, as if we knew each other. Pressured by the line forming behind us for her autograph we parted prematurely, regretfully.

26

THE ENDLESS CIRCLE of obsessiveness is nowhere reserved for clients only. I can attest to this given my own predilection for listening to the same CD over and over again. It would be enough to drive anyone mad had they not the same lovelorn quest. Anita, Anita where art thou? With no word I am at the mercy of this thin flat circle and an invisible laser beam that plays Anita's sweet melancholy with piercing precision. Her woe, now mine, is coupled with the angst of Annie's disappearance and Montana's betrayal. I have nothing to lose. With one last try I compose the following letter in between clients and await her response or the advent of virtual reality. Whichever comes first.

Dear Anita,
Thank you for resting your sweet song on my
eyes. No one ever has before. Feeling the
notes spinning round my corneas made records
out of them both . . .your label, of course. A
splendid infinity seems to connect us behind
the eyes and I am moved by it, by you. If I
could sing, I would sing to you. Instead, I ask:
Will you have dinner with me?
        Sincerely,
        Cloe Goldwin

Snow White

SNOW WHITE'S HAIR was dyed black. Her lipstick, her nail polish, her dress, her cape, and her spirit were also black. But her skin was as white as snow; ghostly white. Snow White was an albino. She lay alone in a deathlike sleep, in a transparent coffin for a week. She overdosed on a gram of coke, too much to drink, and half a bottle of Valium. The iron lung was the closest she came to a mother's grieving breast.

Snow White had wanted to change her life when she came to see me. It was a lonely road for a motherless child. An uncle was her only living relative. She was a small-town girl who took a bite of the Big Apple and was poisoned by the life she could buy with that kiss. At twenty one years old Snow White had no kisses left. She used them up in the House of the Seven Dwarfs. She ate from their plates, slept in their beds and swallowed their cum.

Mirror, mirror on the wall, who is the fairest of us all? A wicked queen mother fashioned Snow White after herself. "Trick Baby, that's what she called me," Snow White recalls in a freeze-dried rage. "I laugh away my pain the way my mother would laugh at me," she comments. The observation makes us both sad, but no tears fall. A month of Tuesdays at 4:00 builds a growing trust. And then a sign of life emerges. First her lipstick: A brick color replaces black, not bright, not red, but still a color. Next, her micro mini grows into a skirt. The skirt is a deep emerald green. With fuck-me pumps transformed to Nike's the transition begins. A sexual object comes to life. Snow White begins to awake. I am hopeful but I keep that to myself.

Snow White has something new to show me. Her words don't come easily, traveling far from tender heart through tissue callused by whippings, rapes, and fucking johns. She sticks out her tongue like an obedient child at the request of a family doctor. A steel stud pierces her tongue. "A metaphor for the pain of putting words to feelings?" I ask.

On the following Tuesday she misses her appointment. When I call her uncle answers. "She has left her body in the corner of the room, leaving the whites of her eyes fixed on a hanging florescent bulb." He takes her to the emergency room where she is hospitalized immediately.

Slipping away, leaving marbles for eyes, she has become a fetal knot that gets tighter with the days. It's not AIDS the doctors say. It's not a hundred other possibilities, but the destruction to her brain is massive. Her white matter is uniformly destroyed. Diagnosis: Unknown. Prognosis: Dismal.

A gargoyle's steel head keeps watch while an unknown tenant assesses its new house. Snow White hasn't the life left in her to take the stud out of her tongue. Doctors in the hospital haven't the guts to try. If she bites them in the process, who knows what they'll get? If they put her to sleep to remove it, who knows if she will ever awake?

Her uncle sits in the same stiff chair from the day before. His eyes are swollen red but he is not without hope. Massaging her relentlessly he fondles her body to stimulate her immune system. It's according to the special readings of a guru whose name he can't pronounce. Three patients in the room, although half dead, have come out of their stupor long enough to ask him to stop. His devotion creates suspicion. The director of the hospital has also demanded that he stop.

Miraculously, several mornings later Snow White opens her eyes. She forms whole sentences but they no longer make sense. Her uncle is convinced he has saved her life. Now empowered healer, he will do more for her when he gets her home. After she is released an aide finds the little steel ball under the bed. The stud had, imperceptibly, loosened its hold on her tongue and lost its head between the sheets. Carelessly, without much thought, the aide throws it in the garbage.

Devoted uncle healer moves in with his niece, now in diapers, for a second time. She is better, but not well. She will never be more than a body that moves slowly. Now he massages her private parts in the privacy of the home he calls "theirs." He has left his girlfriend, faithful to his niece first. Prisoner by candlelight, unkempt and naked she walks through the house but no farther. All calls have stopped, the phone has been disconnected.

I'm told after many days of trying to call that a friend knocked at the door. With no answer, she put her ear to the door and heard the climax of this story. There is no appeal to the proper authorities. The authorities are too proper to interfere based on hearsay. And so, Snow White lives forever after, eternally damned as her uncle's blow doll. "Case closed," says the Bureau for the Disabled.

27

I CONTINUE TO move in and out of reality like sipping a strong drink. Annie's disappearance is hard to swallow. I cannot get the package of fat off my mind. It stays with me as if it were my own fat, equally tenacious. Detective Demson tells me they are on it. "We're following any and every lead. Stay calm," he tells me. I cannot.

Usually the mail comes around 10:00 a.m. This morning it arrived earlier, giving me time to go through it before my first client. With bills and advertisements for cheaper long-distance carriers came a free start-up disk, "Instant Access to the Internet." Everyone is on-line . . . America is on-line. Bargain hunters, lovers, even murderers are surfing the web. Why not a flesh-eating abductor? I insert the CD into the drive and the hunt begins. There is a bulletin board posted for Over Eaters in New York City. It is entitled "Fat Is A Killer, Isn't It?" If Annie's abductor is out there he might respond to that. Under the nickname "Ms. Freud" I place a cryptic message. If he's out there he will get it.

—A Pound of Fat for Thought . . . I am an author and a therapist writing a new book. Seeking personal interviews. Ms. Freud

It takes only a day before I get some responses:

—Write your own book. Fuckoff.
—Chubby charmer are you? Is that all you have to offer? I think too much already (I weigh 300 pounds). Whale.
—You will never get a man that way, honey. You gotta think better of yourself. Elsie

I check the board daily. With more of the same I am about to give up. And then, a suspicious note appears.

—That fat chance awaits you. Meet me on the steps of the Museum of Natural History tomorrow at 6 PM sharp. Wear something red. I'l l find you.
Rolls.

My heart is pumping like a rig that has struck oil. The Museum of Natural History is a curious choice. Immediately, my mind goes to Anastase. The museum was his home, anthropophagy is his profession—and his meal of choice. He has taken the bait. It's Anastase. It must be him. I try to trace the message but he has covered his tracks. I am ready for him, anyway.

I consider calling Demson and then I reconsider. He made it clear he did not want me getting involved. I want to meet "Rolls" face to face. If it is Anastase I can get to him . . . to get to Annie. I know his history. We have a relationship. If I call the police they may botch up the contact I have made. Armed with a tape recorder, a portable phone, and a small can of pepper gas I make my way over to the museum the next evening. There is an exodus of people leaving work from the surrounding buildings. The crowd passing the museum steps makes me feel less alone but not safe. My insides are shaking to the tune of "Goldfinger." The bizarre fantasy of being in a Bond film is rudely interrupted by my own bodily functions. I am dehydrated. My lips are cracking from the stress and I am in sore need of a toilet.

By 6:20 the crowd starts to thin out. I am afraid I have been stood up. I am circling around like a spinning dervish when a figure makes his way out of a shadow. Slowly, he walks toward me from the far side of the steps. My bowels begin to assert themselves as he comes closer. He emerges out of the crowd. I know this man's walk. "What now?" I think to myself. His face takes form as he calls my name, "Cloe?" My bowels relent.

"Detective Demson, what are you doing here?" I polish off the word "here" in a high pitch as if we had just bumped into each other in Bloomingdales.

"Perhaps you can tell me," he says as he focuses on my red windbreaker. "Our encounter is no coincidence, 'Freud.' You overstepped the boundaries."

There is nowhere to hide. I ask, as if apologizing, "Detective, why the museum? I mean why did you choose this one?"

"Just a tip, Freud, 'Sometimes a cigar is just a cigar.' My dentist is on Columbus Avenue—root canal. Now, will you let us handle this case?" My plan is reduced to a bungling cliché from a tacky mystery. "Stick to heads, Cloe and leave the streets to us. You won't get hurt that way."

"I am sorry. It won't happen again. Please, forgive me. It was foolish, crazy really. I think I'll go home now." Headed straight for under my bedcovers, I find consolation only in knowing that even the Internet is covered.

28

I AM IN a tail spin but the show must go on . . .

Group therapy is a mixing of the minds with partic-
ipants who, although out of their own minds, are free to
comment on yours. It is a kind of chicken soup of half-
cooked vegetables suspended in a seasoning of trust that
makes itself better through a mechanism that is not
entirely understood. It is here that we meet. Once a
week, every week at 5:00 p.m. sharp we see how others
see us, what they see in us, and how not to care so much
about what they think, anyway.

Traditionally, the role of a group therapist is that of
a mute back- seat driver, an actively inactive leader with
the non-judgmental facade of a cucumber who dares not
offer her own opinion lest she chance exposure and lead
the group astray. Lucky for me. I can barely speak with
all that is going on.

One by one the group takes form as it has so many
times before. As usual, Mustache Joe, Moshe for short,
arrives early. His yarmulke clings to the top of his head
with the help of a bobby pin probably lent to him by a
"fallen woman." No doubt that is why it must be fas-
tened to his head. I keep the irony to myself.

Ben enters next. "I'm sorry I'm late," he says, "I
was busy cumming. I'm a donor now." Ben is not late.
He apologizes, anyway. It is his way of getting accep-
tance. Moshe placates him by telling him that he's OK
rather than it's OK. He knows what he needs and gives
it freely. They have been in group for almost a year
now. While they wait for the rest of the group to arrive
Ben tells Moshe about a new porno flick he's working
on called *The Harder It Gets.*

Ronald takes his seat on the far side of the room.
Wrestling with the side effects of cross-dressing he pulls

out a hand-held mirror and tries to remove what is left of the silver blue liner around his eyes. He digs into his pocket with his free hand and pulls out a dirty Kleenex, which he spits on like a mother. Furiously, he rubs the Kleenex back and forth over his eyes. Meanwhile, Goldie arrives draped in chinchilla. Neither hook, nor hanger will do. Skins like these command priority seating. First, she fusses with folding them just right. Then she finds just the right place for them . . . on her lap. Finally, Dr. Star arrives at the stroke of 5:00 p.m., followed by Bernard who nervously takes his seat, resting his long nails on the side arm of my couch.

Poor impulse control usually gives Goldie the courage to break the ice. "I'm so upset. I'm so upset. Yesterday my boyfriend gave me a teddy bear."

"So what?" Ben asks.

"Well, if you'd let me finish . . . He lied. Said he bought it especially for me last night."

"How do you know he didn't?" Ben asks.

"Because sometimes I go through his things when he isn't home. I know I shouldn't but the bear and his ex-girlfriend's love letters have been in his top drawer ever since I moved in, more than a month ago."

"How did you deal with it?" Bernard asks clutching the leather cushion he is sitting on.

"I didn't. That's why I'm talking about it. He's gonna know I've been sneakin' through his draws if I bring it up. I'm stuck. This teddy bear's killing me. I look at it and I wanna tear its eyes out, I wanna shove it down his throat . . . I don't know, is being a sneak worse than being a liar? Whadda you think, Doc?"

"Good enough question but it is not about what I think."

"For once, would you just give me an answer?" Goldie whines.

Dr. Star interjects. "What are you really asking for Goldie? Sounds like you want the answer to all the questions no one ever took the time to answer." Dr. Star's comment goes straight to the heart of Goldie. Wounding silence leaves an opening for Ronald to move in. "My wife accuses me of having an affair . . . The only woman I'm seeing is myself—in her clothes."

The group proceeds as usual. Casually, I consider each client of murder.

Heinz

HEINZ IS A new client. He calls panting from the airport to set up an appointment. "Hello Dr. Goldwin, a friend of mine gave me your name a few weeks ago but I was afraid to call. I just missed my plane because I was afraid to get on it. My baggage, however, has no fear. It is, as we speak, on its way to Berlin without me. I was wondering if I could see you before the next flight?"

Heinz is handicapped by a metaphor. Enclosed spaces are brutal mothers from which there is no escape. I agree to see him in two hours. As planned, he rings the downstairs bell and I tell him, from the intercom, that I will be right down to get him. Well, perhaps "right down" is an underestimation. The elevator works on its own time. Especially when it is freezing outside. I swallow what's left of my bacon, lettuce, and tomato sandwich, and I'm off to greet the man whose under-wear is in search of its rightful owner somewhere over the blue skies of Germany.

A gray flannel suit tailored to perfection with his initials embossed on his shirt cuffs introduces Heinz . . . Yet, he cowers as he extends his hand. I'm not quite sure whether he wishes to shake my hand or hold on to it as he steps into the smell of dead meat. One of Mel's customers enters behind him. Cocoa is a friendly drag queen in a red wig and a pink patent leather miniskirt. "I'm just on my way to buy a pair of silk stockings at my favorite store, sweet honeys. And you girls? Time for a new dress?" She directs her gaze to Heinz . . . My professional demeanor is at this moment compromised, smashed really. Nevertheless, I reach out for respect. As the steel door slams shut, I introduce myself to Heinz, who is already in a state of agitated claustropho-bia, with no preparation for the tortured sounds that start with the movement upward. While I try to put Heinz at ease the elevator misses Cocoa's stop. Mel's store sign blurs as we pass it on the way up. Suddenly, the small round window on the inside door has our full attention. It also misses my floor with the same indifference. No surprise to me. Ever so casually, I press the button for the fourth floor again. Ever so casually, Heinz starts to hyperventilate as he inquires if we just missed our floor. The elevator repeats a frantic up and down motion going faster and faster, repeatedly passing the fourth floor as it moans. I press the red button and the alarm sounds off a deafening blast. There's no hiding it now. The three of us are stuck—one Teutonic misanthrope, a flaming dinge queen (black transsexual), and an icon of mental health. Life has a wicked sense of humor, but Heinz has no trace of laugh lines on his face.

Meanwhile, I attempt to use the *in vivo* experience as an opportunity to help Heinz overcome his fear of enclosed places. He is, however, resistant to my slightest utterance. "My feet are coming off girls," Cocoa complains. She removes her gold spike heels and takes a seat on the floor, spreading her legs far apart. Instantly, Heinz and I become transfixed on a run in her stocking which is making its way up from her grossly oversized ankle toward an unseemly bulge at the fork in the road.

Heinz's breathing is timed to that run, like a locomotive sweating steam. I suggest he breathe from a greasy brown bag on the dirty floor to slow down his hyperventilating. Faithful to his nature, he interprets my suggestion as a command and obeys almost instantly. Solicitously, Cocoa extends a pink polka-dot handkerchief to him as he takes a seat next to her on the floor.

Cocoa tries to humor him. She whispers in his ear, "Sure would like to get you breathin' like this at my place sometime, honey."

But to no avail. Originally, my new ex-client was afraid to fly. Now he can't wait. But it's understood—our session will never get off the ground.

29

THE ELEVATOR IS working my nerves, but otherwise not working at all. The situation is serious because of the physical logistics of the floor. The fire escape and the only stairwell to the outside are in Kramer's apartment next door. When the elevator breaks down, the only way out is through their apartment.

Technically, I am their "roommate" even though we do not share apartments. This detail gets them off the hook with the Fire Department. Otherwise, it would be illegal for them to rent half the floor to me without any means of egress, especially when the elevator breaks down. This peculiar arrangement has become a dependable source of anxiety, especially because Rudolph, their attack dog, paces Kramer's apartment freely. When I first moved in I would knock on the door with a doggy biscuit. I hoped to win Rudolph's affection, realizing how important our friendship would be in an emergency. Rudolph, a mean German Shepherd, was only too happy to devour the biscuit first. But his fierce growl made his preference clear. My bones are what he really wants. He does not care to be friends.

Given this hard cold fact, the Kramers and I have an understanding. Under no circumstances are they to leave the floor without tying Rudolph up first. And their door is to be left unlocked at all times. My access to the stairwell is imperative in case the elevator breaks down or there is a fire. It is an in-house law that occasionally gets violated when Steven, their teenage son, has more important things on his mind than my safety.

It is Friday, 5 p.m. sharp, when Anastase rings the bell downstairs for his rite of passage. The fear of ascending malfunction heightens as I ring for the elevator to go downstairs and bring him up. The absence of the usual moans and groans of the aged cables makes it clear. It's not running better. It's not running at all. I call Anastase from the intercom. "Meet me around the other side of the building by the stairwell. The elevator's stuck. I'll be down in a minute to open the side door and let you in."

One knock on Kramer's door and it is understood. The elevator is broken. Steven grabs Rudolph by the collar, holding him back with one hand, opening the door with the other, giving me entrance to the stairwell through his loft. "By the way," he reminds me, "my parents have gone away for the weekend but me and Rudolph will be around, I guess . . . Won't we Rudolph? Rudolph is jealous. He thinks I spend too much time away from him because of my new girlfriend," Steven comments. "I agree with Rudolph on that one, Steven. Rudolph should not be left alone," I emphasize.

After successfully retrieving Anastase from downstairs, we pass back through the Kramers' loft together. Rudolph makes a show of his pearly whites in concert with a ferocious growl, highlighting how tenuous our lives are. Just a split second alone with us. That is all he wants. If not for Steven's hold on Rudolph we would be chopped liver.

Curiously, Anastase shows little fear. He makes light of the impromptu situation with a detached humor once we are back in my office. "Was passing through that lion's den a prelude of what's to come? Thank you for that existential experience. If I didn't need therapy before, I do now. So let's get on with it, Dr. Goldwin."

"I quite understand. Sorry about that, Anastase." I respond awkwardly, fully aware of the unprofessional context, haunted by a familiarity of his stilted manner that I still can't place.

"Now, where did we leave off last week Dr. Goldwin, before we were so rudely interrupted by the expiration of your fifty-minute meter—or was it forty-five minutes? I don't recall."

"It sounds like you have some feelings about the time allotted to our sessions."

"Are you alluding to my profound sense of deprivation, Dr. Goldwin? That eternal gnawing inside of me is perhaps no different than Rudolph's growl. However, my collar is white."

Suddenly, there's a familiar bang . . . Kramer's door slams shut. I can hear it through the wall that separates my office from their loft. The silence catches me off guard. If Steven had remembered to tie up Rudolph before he left, the dog would be howling, at least for a few minutes. I realize there is no exit from the floor, the elevator is broken, and the dog is loose. However shaken, I choose to ignore the fact that we are stranded. Steven will return before the hour is up, I tell myself.

"Are you listening, Dr. Goldwin? That resounding clang just jolted you, didn't it?"

He picks up on everything, I say to myself.

"I am astutely aware, Dr. Goldwin. Have you noticed? You know my mother used to jump like that. But she spent the better part of her youth jumping to the "heil" of Nazis. What is your reason, Doctor? Afraid to be alone with your client?"

His perspicacity unravels me. I fiddle with the papers on my desk and the mail I've yet to open, trying to regain my calm. Then I reflect his observation back. "How does my jumpiness leave you feeling?" I ask, still mining for some kind of emotional core.

"I jumped when my mother jumped. I anticipated her every move. Otherwise, I might get in her way. That would result in . . . well do you believe in corporal punishment, Dr. Goldwin? Physical abuse, I believe is the colloquialism for it these days. Actually, learning to avoid the next blow heightened my intuitive powers. It was how I survived."

"I am struck by your sophistication, Anastase. It is hard for me to believe you have come to your insights in isolation with no prior therapy."

"Are you calling me a liar, Dr. Goldwin? After all, therapy assumes a healing process. Do I appear healed? Are you impressed by my warmth or is it my emotional sensibility? I think not. But then, neither was Claudia. My proto-emotions, I think, was the term she used."

"Claudia? Who was Claudia?"

"Claudia was a woman who called herself a 'therapist.'" The cool flair of his words is impervious, unruffled by the contradiction.

"What was she then?" I ask, chilled by his dark eyes that seem more like holes. Frozen by the thought of no escape.

"She was just another woman, not unlike yourself. Therapists, Dr. Goldwin, are just a subheading, falling under the broader rubric of purchasables, a sacrilegious profession not unlike my mother's. A couch or a bed, either way your legs are open wide. It doesn't matter who I am. I could be anyone. You will understand me, for the right price. Won't you, Dr. Goldwin? And I need understanding desperately. I wasn't lying when I said I was addicted to prostitutes. You can understand why, can't you? That is your business. Tell me, does one go to a therapist to get over their addiction to therapy, Dr. Goldwin?

"It's all about transference, isn't it? You remain a blank slate just long enough for the primal dependency to fester. You are the receptacle for the bloody history of how many lost souls, Dr. Goldwin? Clients are attached to their own fantasies, the ones they project onto you. The resonating 'hums' and 'ahs' all timed to a tale of woe. At last, the all-caring custodian, the mother of mothers, ready to hold one's scars in the safety of her bosom ever so carefully—only until the hour's up, of course." So much the better for perspective.

Alarmed by his aggression in concert with the tent pitched between his legs I attempt a furtive glance at my watch.

"See what I mean, Doc? I still have some time though, don't I? Anyway, one must take what isn't given."

"What do you mean by that?" I ask feeling the danger heighten, knowing I am ensnared.

"You ask for more than you give. I hate that about women, about therapists. You're all the same. Aren't you?"

The ice-cold rage of Anastase's voice scoops the heart out of me as he gets up from the coach and moves slowly toward his tote bag. His steely eyes cut into me. Suddenly, he pulls a knife out nearly as sharp. My life sits on the tip of a blade, reduced to a point of puncture no larger than the dot of an i.

"Anastase, what are you doing?" My heart pounds against my ribs as if it had fists. The organ is a giant trapped inside me. My mouth is paper dry. "What do you want, Anastase? Can we work this through? There must be a way."

"All I know is I want to consume you, destroy you really. It is what consumes me. Can you help me with that, Doc?"

"Let me try. Trust me with it, Anastase."

"Well then, it's not enough to want to taste your private parts, Cloe. I want to swallow them whole. Mm, luscious." He remains comfortably seated as he speaks. "I don't like stomachs, though. They taste clammy, tough to swallow. Don't care for the sludge inside either. I like to do the chewing myself, if you know what I mean. Hearts, now they are superb. Unless, of course they've been broken too many times. Then they're tough, stringy, especially when you eat them raw. Do you have a broken heart, Cloe? Can you imagine what it's like to bite into someone's heart? Still warm. Still pumping. Without missing a beat . . . It is the consummate meal. A gourmet's taste for intimacy has no bounds. Oh, I ache for you Cloe. I have for some time." His index finger rests over the top of the blade. Casually, he waits for just the right moment to turn my flesh into meat. A gourmet does not rush. Now he instills in me the terror he felt as a kid.

A pause extends the reality of our internment. Utter silence congeals the blood in my veins to stone. Numbness fills me empty. Gastronomic exploitation by a loved-starved carnivore. I want to run but I am dog food either way. If not for Anastase, Rudolph would have me.

What happened to Annie? I desperately want to ask but I am afraid it will antagonize him. I am frightened to death. Enraged at the same time. I want to kill him, tear his flesh apart for what he has done to Annie and to the others. And for what he will do to me. But there is no room in this office for more than one cannibal. I have to keep my cool, function as a therapist. My only hope is to sing for my life, like never before, like in Scheherazade.

"I am going to suck your breasts out, Cloe. The succulent rapture of a warm liquid blend . . . blood-milk. Mm, I am in the pink, Cloe. " He stares at me with a cool smile.

Anastase is morally insane. He is a psychopath. Desperately, I try to come up with a way of dealing with him. Fantasies of attacking the breast are attacks on the mother's insides, as if the breast deliberately refused to provide gratification to Baby Blue. Melanie Klein is his favorite analyst because she understands him. Anastase is an infant envious of the mother because she controlled the flow of nourishment. Female therapists are frustrating mother . . . the whore mother—and my number is up. Haunting photos of human carnage at a tender age, his early exposure to abuse and mutilation, his identification with flesh-eating dinosaurs. Sadism comes natural. Frustrated, he steals the love that was not given.

Anastase also envies therapists, I continue to reason. He is humiliated by interpretations he didn't think of himself. He defends against his envy by denigrating them. It is how he makes himself feel self-sufficient, omnipotent, above his own needs. It's a form of denial. And then it comes to me.

"Anastase, I have an idea."

"What could that possibly be, Dr. Feelgood?"

I ignore his sarcasm. I am in no position to make interpretations that might anger him . . . except for one. With a deep breath I take the chance. "Anastase, you want to consume me to become me to get the good stuff without the dependence." He listens for the moment and I continue. "Let me give you that. Switch roles with me."

"What? I despise you, Doctor," he snarls rolling the r of doctor around on the tip of his tongue. "You're a hoax, an apocryphal. You don't make the sick well. You're no different from a religious zealot, a pseudo-scientist. You are just as lost in this world as me. Well, perhaps not quite . . . What is your favorite cut, anyway, Cloe? I prefer breast meat myself. Might give you a sampling of your own . . . if you'd like, mm? Juicy."

"Anastase, there is more than one way to skin a cat." The cliché sickens me. "Feed yourself. Find a space inside my role that's safe. Just try it."

"That is an interesting idea Cloe. Yes, Cloe. I like the way it sounds. I will devour your role first, then your flesh. The foreplay excites me. Stand up then. We will switch seats as well. Take the couch." Anastase moves toward my chair leaving his open tote bag on the side of the couch.

"Let's begin then, starting with your name and some basic demographics for a proper history." He takes on the role with an air of credibility. All right begin."

"My name is Anastase Wright and . . ."

"Oh no, that is not the deal," he interrupts, waving

his knife in the air as if it were a conductor's baton. "Anastase Wright is the therapist now. Cloe Goldwin is the client. I won't let you hide behind my story, Cloe. It's yours I want."

That was not the deal I had in mind. However, the vulnerability of being analyzed, turned inside out by a madman is more appealing than being eviscerated by him. If he sees me as another therapist . . . a lifeless, odorless, objective nonentity with no past and no present, it might be easier for him to kill me. But, if I stretch my stories out, perhaps I can become a real person to him, not an object. It is my only hope . . . at least until Steven gets back—then, I might have a chance to escape.

"Start with your mother, Cloe. That is the beginning, isn't it?" He clips his words the way some cut nails. Short.

"Actually, my grandmother brought me up for the, the . . . first three, for the first three years."

"You're stuttering, Cloe. Why did your grandmother bring you up?"

"When I was born my mother suffered from postpartum depression."

"For three years? You are leaving something out. I want to know the details, Cloe. Unless of course, you don't have the stomach to make the switch. I have the stomach, Cloe. I quite like my new profession. Now get on with the truth before I cut it out of you." He unsheathes my role as therapist as if he were slicing it away. It leaves me undone but I have no choice. "My mother was hospitalized . . ."

"For what, Cloe? Please don't make me ask you again."

"She tried to jump out of a hospital window after I was born."

"I see. Doesn't sound like she was too glad to have you. How come, Cloe?"

"My mother had a rough childhood."

"Don't stop. Unless, you want to eat early?"

"When my mother was six, my grandmother had postpartum depression, also. 'Milk poisoning.' That's what they called it then. My mother told me how she hid under the dining room table with her younger brother. She clutched onto him while she watched my grandmother struggle with two Goliaths dressed like ice cream men. The giants buckled my grandmother up from behind. They didn't care how loud she screamed or how hard she was crying. Her arms were tied up and she couldn't move. Then the giants pulled her out onto the streets. All the neighbors were watching as my grandmother desperately tried to free herself from the straitjacket. Some of the kids on the block laughed as my mother screamed "Mommie!" The men shoved my grandmother into a big white truck with flashing red lights. It looked like the ice cream truck that always came by their house. She ran after the white truck until she was out of breath. The sirens and flashing lights faded into the distance with her mother."

"What happened then? I'm waiting." Engrossed, Anastase tightens his grip on the knife.

"She didn't see my grandmother for seven years. My mother grew old in an orphanage. She was repeatedly raped in that orphanage. By the time her mother came home my mother was worn out from her childhood.

"As a little girl my mother would ask for more bread at the dinner table, as if she were still in the orphanage. 'You don't need permission to take a piece of bread anymore, my daughter. You are home now.' My grandmother would remind her."

Anastase listens as if he cared. I wonder if he is capable of empathy or just feigning it. "Get back to your grandmother. I never had a grandmother," he demands, using the tip of the knife to clean under his nails. My wondering stops.

"I have vague memories of lying in a hammock swinging between two tall trees. My grandmother would stand in front of an old wooden easel. She looked the way grandmothers used to look. She was a Jewish immigrant from Russia; full-bodied and warmhearted. The yard seemed like a wild jungle. Actually, it was a small garden on the side of the house. She painted rather than pulled weeds she would say. The smell of wildflowers was inseparable from the scent of oil paint. 'It's time for your nap,' she would remind me. Already suspended in a sensory solution of turpentine and paint I took the leap willingly. I fell asleep to the hush of brushes to canvas."

"How nice to be lulled to sleep by the sound of brushes as opposed to a tortured fairy tale or some sucker cumming in the next room . . . Oh, but I am sorry, Cloe. Go on."

"My grandmother used to paint below the house in a musty basement that smelled like a rat, impossible to find but forever dying. Her son had returned after studying fine art at the Sorbonne in Paris. He stored his paintings in that basement. It took him many months to persuade Betty Parsons to see his work. Betty Parsons was the first dealer to exhibit Jackson Pollock. Anyway, he took Betty down there to show her his paintings when she was struck by one in particular. 'What about this one?' she asked. 'It's not so self-conscious like the rest. It's honest, passionate. It's great.'"

"The painting wasn't his. Humiliated, he called Hanna—that was my grandmother—downstairs from the kitchen. 'Mama, do you know anything about this painting?' He questioned her with a show of self-control that was a lie. He had a mean temper. Quietly, in broken English, Hanna confessed: 'It's mine. I'm afraid to say so. Mit de pent dat you throw avay, mit de tubes dat you throw in de garbage I pent. At de night some-times vhen you sleep I do some pictures, in the day ven you go out, just to pass de time I pent . . . de oders are in de shack mit the tools. I vas afraid you and your fader vould make fun. I never study. I just do to do, mit the left overs.'"

"I like that, Cloe. More. I want more of your grand-mother." He waves the knife back and forth at me. The silverware in his hand makes me cringe. I can only hope my cellulite ruins the meal. He will see the fat sagging on my body and recoil, unable to ever eat again . . . But for now I must pacify him. "Hanna was afraid the fam-ily would ridicule her. After all—who was she to paint? She saw herself as an immigrant who could hardly speak English, with no education, with no training, a prior mental patient who was released but not replen-ished. They made fun of her English but she wouldn't let them make fun of her painting. Her son was the 'artist.' She just painted.

"Betty Parsons wasn't laughing though. She wanted to know who painted this picture. That was enough for Hanna. She would never be institutionalized again. Not after she found art. Not after Betty Parsons found her. She painted the pain out of painting . . . 'Art makes a gift out of sadness. It gives it meaning,' she would say in her way. 'Some believe in god. I believe in art'"

"And your grandfather, Cloe—what was he like?" Anastase asks almost like a friend. "I never had a grandfather," he recalls. Getting up he takes a seat next to me on the couch and scratches a speck of dust off my sweater with the point of his knife, as if it were a show of affection.

I continue with whatever comes out of my mouth. I am too frightened to make up stories. I can only draw on the past. "The Dow Jones was the barometer of my grandfather's mental health. When it was up, 'Philip Morris'—that was what my father called him—was a chipper fellow with a cigar in his mouth and a good joke. When the Dow was down so was he. 'Overly invested' was the phrase I recall my parents using.

"One year, when the Dow was bottoming out, I think it was in 1957, he came to live with us. My mother arranged for him to sleep in my room. His bed was placed against the wall opposite mine and every night for six months I would dread the inevitable . . . the smell of his socks. I held my breath as I watched him take his shoes off." Anastase and I laugh half a laugh each. "Then I hid under the pillows to muffle the sound of his cries. But it was unavoidable. Eventually, I would come out from under the pillows and find him banging his head against the wall, wailing about the declining prices of his stocks. At the time, I was only eight, I couldn't figure out why he repeated the same fractions every night with such sadness. The smaller the numbers, the more upset he became. Once, I went over to his bed to try to talk to him. 'Grandpa,' I asked, 'why does two-and-a-quarter make you so sad?' My grandfather wept, 'Child, corrections are bad, corrections are mistakes. Now go to bed!'

"It's not surprising I got an unsatisfactory in math that year. Mrs. Roman, my third grade teacher, wrote in my report card:

Cloe's attitude toward math is poor. She does not take corrections well. She is traumatized by fractions and her ability to convert them into decimals is damn near impossible . . .

"Madness or art; your choices were rigged from the beginning, Cloe. Obviously you chose art but not without madness, I can tell."

The depth of Anastase's perception sways me for the moment. He is not entirely without an ability to feel, I think to myself when he slices a button off my blouse with a quick turn of his wrist. Then, he holds the blade straight at me. "And your father. What about him?" He snarls.

"We weren't close. I was my mother's daughter. I mean, he was a simple man with simple tastes. He wanted me to be a secretary. I worked my way through school but when I needed his help he resented it. He resented me. When I was a kid I was afraid of him. "

"Afraid of him, how come?"

"I'm not sure."

"Cloe, if you avoid my questions I'll have to switch roles again from a therapist to a psychopath. Which do you prefer, dear? Continue." He cuts off another button. This one exposes my bra. I imagine him sucking on my bones . . .

"When my mother would leave the house he would beat me. Finally, she discovered the welts on my body. I was five then. She threatened to leave him if he ever raised his hand to me again. He never did. But his attitude never changed. Maybe he was jealous. I think he competed with me for my mother's love. He was like a child."

"Are you sure that was the reason, Cloe?" He asks with a sardonic smile.

"What do you mean?"

"Your mother tries to kill herself when you're born . . . Your father hated you from the beginning . . . He beat you, right? Did your mother kiss the milkman, Cloe?" He draws out the words slowly and then chuckles.

I am shaken. I never doubted that I was my father's daughter until now. But it makes sense. For the moment, I am silent, introspective. But, he is chewing on my soul, ravenous for every detail. Curiously, Anastase has liberated me from a father that never was one.

"Tell me what made you become a therapist, Cloe." Anastase pushes on while he cleans between his teeth with the point of his knife.

I feel like I am in a pressure cooker. I cooperate, not wanting to intensify his hunger. It is quiet next door. There is no sign Steven has returned.

"From the time I was a child my fascination went toward the macabre. I didn't want to explore outer space. It was inner space that fascinated me. I was a psychonaut, sort of speak. I wanted more than anything to visit an insane asylum, ideally with someone in it I knew, someone who had lost their mind. I wanted to see people inside out. At night when the room was dark I would imagine being in a jungle of lost minds that had no attachment to their owners. Webs of tangled hair, wild limbs, knotted memories moving to the sound of shooting bile, raging in and out of sanity. That was the ultimate adventure."

"You wanted to see what your mother and your grandmother and your grandfather were like when they were mad, didn't you Cloe?"

His insight catches me off guard again. There is nowhere to hide.

"Continue, Cloe."

"One day when I was eleven my wish came true. My best friend Julie stopped calling for me. I didn't know why. Her parents would not answer the door when I knocked, and I knocked every morning for a month of mornings. Finally one night she called. 'Where are you, Julie? Where have you been?' I asked desperate, swollen inside from missing her. She spoke slowly, with a drawl that was unfamiliar to me. It was hard for me to understand what she was saying. It sounded like, 'Cloe I'm...please come.' The last word I heard her say was 'Seedlings' before the phone was left dangling." Seedlings was a mental institution. My heart is pounding, drumming out each word as Anastase sits next to me riveted to my stories like the little boy who listened to his mother's gruesome accounts of the Holocaust. "Please, go on. I want more, Cloe."

"It was a cold Saturday morning. Ordinarily, we would already be on our bikes trying to get lost in the neighborhood. I took the bus down Union Turnpike and walked off the main road to the huge buildings with the bars on the windows. I had heard my parents talk about these buildings when we passed them in the car, but never with enough detail for me to know what to expect. The dark mystery of visiting a mental institution at the age of thirteen was fused with fear and longing. It had been weeks since Julie's call. It took that long to get permission from my mother and her mother and the hospital to see her.

"I was ushered onto the floor by a big friendly nurse who knew my name. As she spoke I inhaled the decay of human spirit. 'Julie will be so happy to see you,' she reassured me. Now seasick from the stench, I held waves of my breakfast back. 'She talks about you all the time,' she said. 'Don't be upset about your friend's hair,' the nurse told me. 'Julie did it herself. She pulls it herself. It'll grow back. Don't give it a second thought dear,' she said nonchalantly. I knew my friend was on the other side of the heavy steel door with the tiny window, but the nurse had to find the right key first. 'There are many wards like this one,' she pointed out. One by one, she tried each key. My heart was pounding then the way it is now. Finally, she found it and the steel door swung open.

"My heart moved in gulps as I passed through waves of kids gone bad like rotten fruit. Wading through torn people and the rancid smell of rotting minds I looked for her. Nestled in a dark, isolated antechamber at the end of a hallway sat an old woman with a girl's face. Julie was slumped in a chair, drowning in the moans of a hundred broken dolls whirling around her. Her eyes were pools of muddy water surrounded by the ripples of time. She was only eleven years old. There was the bald spot in the center of her head the nurse warned me about. The rawness of it made me feel ashamed. I looked away from the hole on the top of her head. That was what it looked like.

"Don't stop now, Cloe. Tell me more about your visit." Anastase slits my bra down the middle with the point of his knife. Like skinning a fish he peels off each cup with his fingers.

Shaking, I sing for my life with a vibrato that does not let up. "Julie," I couldn't wait to say it. I shouted it from the top of my lungs. But her name sat at the bottom of my stomach. I couldn't say a word. Half closed, her eyes were different, as if she didn't care about seeing anymore. She made no effort to say 'Hi.' Quietly, I waited. It was a moment longer than any hour. Then, finally, in slow motion she prepared to greet me with a smile . . . a sagging smile, purulent, soaked in a whitish froth like soured milk. The smile had no owner.

"I left Julie that day as I imagined she had left herself. I stored her original smile in a soft safe. The other smile, the sick smile, attached itself to my curiosity and the desire to reach into that dark spot behind the eyes where my friend hid. I'll always wonder what happened to Julie."

"Still looking for Julie are you? Can you see her in my eyes, Cloe, mm?" This time he starts on my thigh. Slowly, with the point of his knife, he unsheathes the slacks off my left leg, barely piercing my skin. "Yummy." His iced rage can give way at any moment to a lethal cut. I offered one intimacy after another. My soul slit open, the rest is his to take. I am a hair away from being eviscerated.

"Now, the best part for last, Cloe . . . your love life."

"I am unable to speak, Anastase. I just can't."

"I said your love life, Cloe. You don't want me to take it from you, now, do you? Don't be afraid. Sex is just a little death. It can't compare to the bliss of eternity."

Careful not to provoke him I start again. "Let me preface what follows with a footnote. I do not pretend to be the paragon of mental health. However flawed, I function as a therapist by virtue of my training, my vantage, and the abysmal state of the art market." Suddenly, I have a second breath.

"I see. I wish you had provided that qualification initially. But then, how many shrinks would be in business if their own lives were the standard of measurement for mental health. Continue Cloe. I want to know how you fucked your relationships up. Now undress yourself before I make you take all your clothes off." He holds his knife between his legs.

"I am gay with a series of false starts I call my love affairs. I have been involved . . . no, in love with a woman, more than one, who ultimately chose a man. Perhaps, they loved me. Perhaps, not. Perhaps the difference between us was the difference between joy and fun. Joy for me, fun for them. Anyway, the more they pulled back the more frustrated I became. . . If you want love give someone your heart. If you want obsession take it away. My need to possess, to consume, to control . . . took over. I became obsessed."

"Sounds like you fall in love with women who are unavailable to you from the beginning. You set yourself up to recreate your father's rejection so you can turn that story around, to give it a happy ending. That your father didn't love you wasn't your fault. But you take the guilt on. It drives the pattern of your unfortunate choices. Why not let it go, Cloe?"

"Your observations are astute, Anastase." He grins with this acknowledgement.

"Thank you, Cloe," he says as he puts his hand on the bare skin of my thigh. "My, it is past the fifty-minute hour, isn't it? It's almost midnight but I want to give you all the time I have, Cloe . . . a marathon session of the blind leading the blind. I am struck by your ambivalence regarding intimacy though. You live vicariously through your clients. You feed off their pain and their pleasure. You attempt to consume your lovers.

I am a cannibal of the flesh, Cloe, but you are a cannibal of the soul. The difference between us is only one of gradation."

Fatigued and almost naked, the fear of provoking him diminishes as if I had nothing to lose. "Your analogy is not unjustified. That I live through my clients, that I am controlling, perhaps consuming may well be true. However, I am a vegetarian."

"Ah, you're getting defensive, Cloe. I've pressed one of your buttons. That gratifies me. I like this, Cloe. It's well . . . juicy." After a moment's silence Anastase starts to sharpen his knife against the steel frame of the desk. "Did you know some tribal mothers like the Chavantes in Uruguay ate their children to recover their strength lost during childbirth? They felt they were entitled to take back what they gave. Some spiders even eat their mothers when they get old. It's called gerontology."

"Is that what you are, Anastase? Are you that spider? Is each therapist you dismember the whore mother who was never there for you?"

"However twisted it is . . . however twisted I am, cannibalism is an attempt at restoration. Pre-Columbian Aztec consumption rituals, pantheistic cults, Dionysian rites, resurrected deities, headhunters, vampires . . . there have been whole cultures in need of a good feed. Any God-eating Catholic will tell you it's Christ's flesh and blood they taste with the sacrament. If you disagree and say 'Hey, get real, it's just bread and wine, you hungry bastard,' they'll scorn you as a heretic. The Eucharist is not a symbolic event. Transubstantiation is pure unequivocal cannibalism. It is an affirmation of life. The earliest forms of analysis are rooted in it. Absolution is its predecessor. Through time there has always been some guy with a graveyard in his stomach. Like Jeffrey Dahmer, like Chikatilo. . . I am one of those guys."

"Does a full stomach fill an empty heart?"

"As if awareness were the answer, Cloe. After Oedipus realized he fucked his mother he tore his eyes out. Insight doesn't mean change, regardless of what your friend Freud says."

"Is that how you justify your murders, Anastase? Are you tearing your eyes out by killing me, by killing the other therapists? Am I your eyes? If so, let me help you see."

"You just want to save your life, Cloe. You don't give a damn about me."

"Anastase, I don't pretend to know the state of desperation that drives you to hack up a woman's body, to swallow her innards like clams, to eat her raw . . . try to touch me with it. What does it feel like to be Anastase Wright?"

"And if I said you could go now, Cloe would you still want to know?"

I consider his question with the gravest concern. Suddenly I hear a bang. Steven is home. At that moment Anastase places his knife on the side of the couch . . . Maybe it's a ploy but it is my only chance.

"If you stay," Anastase whispers, "I could tell you the story your mother told you every night just before you went to bed about two dogs, Lulu and Sigmund. Your mother looked like you, didn't she, Cloe. . . ?"

My chest squeezes at my heart as if it were strangling it. How did he know about Lulu and Sigmund? "My god, finally . . . I recognize your voice. You were my neighbor when I lived in the brownstone on Perry Street!"

Within minutes the door slams again. I wait to hear the beast howl . . . But, silence follows. Steven has left Rudolph unleashed, for a second time. I second-guess myself. Could I have escaped? Did I choose to stay with this madman for closure or was it fear?

"You must like Greek tragedies, Cloe. It is your

fatal flaw. Perhaps, the one that doesn't set you free. Then again, you may well set me free. The night is young . . ." He implies I chose to stay. A sardonic calm smoothes his smile.

"Gordon? That is your real name, isn't it? Gordon Harcourt. All those late night phone calls . . .You were listening to all my conversations, weren't you?"

"Well, that's what vents are for, aren't they? Of course, I thought you were an artist at the beginning." He says, raising his knife like a stylist assessing the wave of my hair. I could let you live if you were an artist. But then I found a psychology journal on the floor in the laundry room. It was addressed to 'Dr. Cloe Goldwin.' Well, you know how I feel about therapists, Cloe. It was late. No one was around. I got my knife and waited behind the garbage pails. Finally, you returned to put your clothes in the dryer. At least, I assumed it was you . . .Well, we all make mistakes, don't we Cloe?" He frowns. "It was too late by the time I got my dinner home, even though I only lived next door. The meat was not as sweet as I had hoped. A remnant of a driver's license was stuck in between my teeth. It indicated I had the wrong dish."

Anastase, No Gordon, had lived under me, like a maggot. He slept in between my sheets with the ceiling between us. I am blind with disbelief. He disarticulated our neighbor in the laundry room, thinking it was me . . . my blood is frozen. I did the laundry that evening but had a hectic day. I remember looking for the journal. By the time I realized I misplaced it I couldn't remember where I left. The police reminded me with the news of Greta's murder.

Circling around me, he makes small talk as a prelude to his first cut. "Ever go to NYU, Cloe? By the way, Anastase Wright really is a professor of Anthropophagy at New York University. I sat in on one of his classes . . ." Now face to face, he raises his knife to my breast as if to slice tuna. "Mm." Ever so casually, he slices off the tiniest tip of my left nipple. Blood red gushes forth edged on a brush of steel. He stands back for just a moment, like a painter angles for perspective. "Oh, blood milk red. Lick it off! Open your mouth or I'll open it for you." He places the side of the blade on my tongue. Taste irony?"

"I taste nothing. I feel nothing." My cries are silent. He goes for the lobe of my ear, slicing off enough of it to make me sick . . . He is deaf with no soul to hear. The last I will know of life is pain so profound it has robbed me of all memories. How perverse my pain is the closest he comes to feeling.

"Up from the floor now, Cloe. It's time to eat. Move." I raise myself from a grave to one that gets deeper.

He escorts me into the kitchen. "Now, get the plates and set the table." The soul of me is dripping away. Gordon takes his place at the kitchen table with his knife at the side of his plate, where it should be. He places the slice of my ear lobe on my plate and the tip of my nipple on his. "Eat your words, Cloe.

I recoil and vomit. "Come now. That's how an analytic silence tastes . . . Not very juicy, is it? Eat it, anyway." He raises my nipple to his lips on a fork. "Mm, guess I got the better dish," he laughs. "Don't worry we will have more to eat later. The night is young."

Pointing to the fridge he motions to get up. Standing behind me with his knife placed ever so gently at my neck we examine the inner contents of my fridge. "There's not much here," he whispers in my ear. My blood covers his face red as he eyes my pubic bone as an alternative.

"Oh, here's some chicken," I exclaim thankful for the discovery. I am still facing the fridge when he moves against me, rubbing his erect genital up and down my buttocks. I shiver, sweating blood. Each breath he draws goes through my lungs. Suddenly, I remember his visit to the clinic for premature ejaculation. The secret knowledge is of little consolation to me now. To recall it would mean my premature death.

"Would you make me a chicken sandwich, Cloe? I love chicken sandwiches so much. I have a special place for them in my heart. Would you put some mayo on it, please. And oh, some lettuce if you don't mind? Yum."

At once I realize Gordon is regressing. He is no longer the intellectual advocate of "anthropophagy" but a hungry little boy. I don't usually have chicken around (unsavory associations) but I made chicken this week for a friend who loves it. I could not eat the little bird's dried-up parts—its wings or its breast and filled up with mashed potatoes instead. I pull out the leftovers with affection. With his blade fully erect and against me, I craft his sandwich to perfection. Each tender filet handled with newfound respect, placed with the utmost care next to its twin on—Oh god, there is no more bread . . . !

"Gordon, I must make your sandwich on an English muffin. Is that OK?" He nods with approval. There is no holding back on the mayo here. Cholesterol is not the issue. The unctuous flow follows a smooth curve when I realize the wasted potential of my butter knife. I have neither the physical stamina nor the heart to use it, even in my own defense.

He sits silently waiting to be served. "You know when I was a kid chicken sandwiches were my favorite. Sammy, the guard at the museum, would eat with me. His bones and the squiggles of his veins showed through his skin like it was wax paper. He had the same station in the Great Hall of Dinosaurs for twenty years. He was kind to me when no one else was. He was my only friend. He looked out for me like the father I never had. Every day he would wait for me to finish school before he took his break to share his chicken sandwich with me. A long dark tunnel under the museum led to the basement storeroom where we ate. The bones of time filled the halls. My nostrils flared to suck in the ancient dust that spiced my half sandwich. We sat together in between huge limbs the size of craters hanging on steel racks from the floor to the ceiling, the room filled with parts of giants distilled from a lost epoch, one Coke between us, just Sammy, me, and the beginning of time. Like I was the future, that was when I still trusted."

"And now, Gordon?" I ask as I hand him his sandwich.

"And now I want to cry, but I am incapable. Sammy talked to me about life in that storeroom, about the birds and the bees, about love, a lot about dinosaurs. There wasn't anything he could tell me about sex that I didn't know but I let him think he could. He knew I didn't have a father but he didn't know I grew up in a cat house. I never told Sammy about my mother. I was too ashamed. I told him she died and I lived with a sick aunt. Then one night it happened . . ."

"What happened, Gordon?"

"Madam Regina knocked on my door. It was about 9:00 p.m. I knew her knock. It was a bang with no apology necessary. My mother never knew Regina called on me to perform sexual acts. She was too busy servicing her johns. 'Gordon, come into my room. I require your assistance.' I did as she asked. I had no choice. It was understood, one of her johns desired the touch of a young boy. Quickly, I slipped into my jeans and walked down the hall to her room. I knocked on her door and then . . . " A tear falls from the side of Gordon's eye.

"What happened, Gordon? Tell me what happened."

"As I opened the door I saw an old man leaning against the brass head-board naked, his white skinny legs spread apart, his cock ready to be mouthed . . . It was Sammy. He looked straight at me, then turned away. Neither of us could hide. I ran from the room with nowhere to go. I never went back to the museum. Never." Gordon breaks down. Moaning, wailing . . .

At last we are both free, I think to myself but what about Annie? In the midst of his sobbing I notice his open tote bag. There, protruding from the zipper is a bone bleached white, maybe an arm. Maybe Annie's, or one of the others. I grab it as if taking Annie's hand and run for my life.

Quivering, I open Kramer's door. Rudolph jumps out from the other end of the loft. He growls hard and loud as he moves toward me. Deliberately he makes a show of his jagged spears. His fangs glow in my face. Shaking, I vibrate like a crystal glass about to crack. With one quick snap of his jaws Rudolph grabs hold of my wrist and turns it crimson red. At first, I use the bone to fight him off. Then he grabs hold of it, biting into it instead of me. I rush past him and through the loft to the stairwell, down the stairs, onto the street.

30

A PINK THONG, coordinated to a chartreuse bustier, fills in the crack between naked buns. Hookers swarm the street crowned in opalescent faces six feet high. I catch their eye and they offer to help. One takes time off from her corner post, leaving behind a sign that reads "Early Bird Specials." Till now we have been familiar strangers. She wraps me in a yellow satin gown with rhinestones that drags along the sidewalk. "Here honey, just don't you worry. I got johns that done the same to me."

"Please call Detective Jack Demson at One Police Plaza. It's an emergency. Tell him to get over here right away. Please, hurry." More than fifteen minutes go by before the police arrive while we wait in the Hole in One, an all-night bagel shop next door. Finally, Demson arrives. He insists I get into the ambulance but I refuse. I must see this nightmare to its end.

Wrapped in the yellow gown, now with red polka dots I make my way back up the stairs. The police gas Rudolph for a period of time all too temporary for my own taste in order to get through to my loft. Upon entering, a blaring CD fills the space with a sad melancholy song. Although familiar I can't place it. I am too frazzled, my nerves unsheathed, myelin free. Gordon sits behind a pile of garbage on the desk. He has opened what is already yesterday's mail. Dressed in silk lingerie that I save for the right occasion, my lace bra and panties fit snugly around his hairy torso. My blood is his rouge. From behind broken bars of dripping mascara a lost child greets us.

Willie, another client, sits opposite him on the couch obediently waiting for his session to begin. Apparently, he does not find Gordon an unreasonable substitute. The elevator must have been fixed during our marathon session. While I was waiting for the police in the bagel shop, one of Mel's salesmen dropped Willie off on the floor. The police did not bother to check the elevator assuming it was still broken.

Suddenly, I recognize the singer in the background. It is Anita Amoricci from the Algonquin Hotel. "Anita Amoricci," I sing to myself. She sent her new CD to me in response to my letter. "You'd Be So Nice To Come Home To" is the only sound I hear.

31

WHEN YOU'RE IN the business of understanding, "good guys" and "bad guys" are just in Westerns. Life is more complex than that. Held captive in my own office, brought to the catacombs of my soul by a client bereft of a soul, Anastase had turned my life inside out. Forced out of my own skin by a madman, anything was possible now.

It was the Sunday morning after. I had no peace of mind. Thankful to be alive I feel guilty about surviving. There is no word of Annie. Gordon admits killing and dismembering two missing therapists, but not Annie. There is hope that she is still alive, unless he is lying.

Midafternoon the phone rings. "Cloe." My heart stops. "You are the first one I'm calling. I just got back . . . Are you there Cloe?" Her voice brings me to life.

"Annie? Is that you, Annie? God, where are you? What happened to you? I have been sick thinking you were dead."

"Dead? You are a drama queen. I'm sorry I didn't tell you I was going away but I wanted to surprise you. I hope you're not angry."

"Surprise me? That you are alive surprises me. Each day has been a month. Where have you been, Annie?"

"You won't believe this but . . . are you ready? I went to The Sun Spa in Colorado to recover. It's a new me. No, an old me . . . I mean the body I used to have."

"To recover? I don't understand. What are you talking about Annie?"

"For seaweed applications after the surgery . . ."

"Surgery?"

"Cloe, I had liposuction. My hips, my thighs, even my

pancake breasts have been renewed, refurbished . . ." She can barely contain her enthusiasm.

I am dazed. "What about the package, Annie, the pound of fat, the letter?"

"Oh, I guess Curt told you. He took everything from me—the bastard . . . my heart, my youth, my money. He tried to control my every move. What I wore and how I wore it. Who I spoke to and what I said. He tortured me . . . drained me dry. Now he has what's left of the old me . . . my fat. Do you think it was an awful thing to do to? I hope so. It lightened me up . . ." Annie is exuberant.

I pause. "Well, I lost a little weight, too. Actually you had something to do with it."

"Really?" Annie's curiosity is peaked. "How much did you lose?"

"Just a little, actually very little . . ." Silence bridges the gap between us.

"Uh, well where did you lose it, Cloe?"

"You want to know where, Annie? Come on over, I'll show you where . . . And then, if you can still eat, I'll serve you some leftovers."

The Meat Market isn't just another neighborhood. It is a state of mind. It's a crack in the veneer, a place where we give a smell to feeling different, then try to hide it West of everything we fear

A hamburger is a hamburger, is the fat lady's thighs . . . and the chicken's head is just around the corner. Knowing someone is a passive happening but understanding is an act of love. Full circles are a satisfying geometry, though, having come this way before. What was will never be again. Again and Again . . . At least that's how I remember it.